About the Author

While I was growing up, my father was in the RAF. This meant that every two years our family would pack up and move to another RAF base. As you can imagine I had plenty of schools before the last one friends – most of whom I got to know

One of the things I during my childhood were the stories I used from the local library. Even if we'd ended up in some remote desert air force station, I always knew that a book could take me into a world filled with people trying to sort out problems often ten times more interesting than my own.

I've written stories and poems since then. Sometimes based on things that have happened to me, sometimes on topics that I'm just interested in. The ideas grow from small incidents – people moving house, starting a new school – which can be transformed into something exciting by simply applying the magic question:

'What if—?'

Nick Manns

Nick Manns' debut novel, *Control-Shift* was short-listed for the North East Book Award and published to wide-spread acclaim.

SEED TIME

Nick Manns

Hodder
Children's
Books

A division of Hodder Headline Limited

A Catalogue record for this book is available from
the British Library

ISBN 0 340 80570 6

Typeset by Avon Dataset Ltd, Bidford-on-Avon, Warks

Printed and bound in Great Britain by
The Guernsey Press Co. Ltd, St Ives plc

Hodder Children's Books
A Division of Hodder Headline Limited
Road
London NW1 3BH

For
Ellie and Harvey

The silver springs grown naked dykes
Scarce own a bunch of rushes
When grain got high the tasteless tykes
Grubbed up trees, banks, and bushes
And me, they turned me inside out
For sand and grit and stones
And turned my old green hills about
And pikt my very bones

John Clare
The Lament of Swordy Well

One

'Right boys, what are you two up to?'

He walked from the patrol car, tugging his uniform straight. A big man with a loose stride, a smile around his mouth and a direct look in his eyes.

'Out for a ride,' said Michael. Easy, effortless, smiling back. And then: 'Part of a school project.'

'And which school might that be?' said the officer, still smiling.

Tony noticed the silver buttons at the front, the black of the material, the number 391 on his shoulders. A moustache neatly trimmed, dark against his brown skin.

They were silent, astride their bikes, abreast. The blue lights on the car flashing a warning.

'So, boys, it's a Friday afternoon and term hasn't ended round here, so what's going on?'

He opened his top left-hand pocket and removed a notebook and pen.

We haven't practised this, thought Tony. We need to talk this through.

Five minutes out of Elton and just past the stone bridge across the river. They'd stood there, looking down at the weed, green and glistening, being pulled in the current, like the hair of someone dead. Trout hanging in the water, pointing upstream.

The road bordered with hawthorn, blackthorn, elder. Trimmed for the summer. Cars every ten minutes. Now this.

'Well then,' said the officer. 'Let's have your names.' The light wind lifting his brown hair.

'Colin Smith,' said Michael promptly. 'And this is . . .'

'It's OK.' The smile had gone. 'He can speak for himself, "Colin". OK son, what's your name?'

He could hear, in some other world, the honking call of geese, and he knew that if he turned his head he would see the V-shape crossing the river behind. They would look down and see the landscape patterned differently from the map Michael had stuffed in his rucksack.

'Yes?' and he realised the officer had asked him a question. Michael was looking at him sharply, his grey eyes telling him to make the speech with craft.

'David,' he said.

' "David",' wrote down the officer, 'and the rest. David what?'

There were reeds fringing the water, like great pale strands of grass. 'Marsh,' he added. 'David Marsh.'

'So,' said the policeman. 'We've got Colin Smith – that's you' – pointing at Michael – 'and – let me see – "David Marsh", out in the middle of nowhere on some kind of school project.' He paused and frowned, the grumble of a tractor beyond the hedge filling the silence.

'So, Colin – or is it David?' – looking at Michael – 'what school have you come from? Would that be Wansford Upper? Stilton Community College? Or are you from one of the schools in Peterborough?'

He realised that this policeman wasn't in any hurry and that sooner or later he was going to check with his station and pass on their details and that then they'd be taken to some strange interview room, separated and questioned. And nothing had been prepared. Their stories would go in different directions almost immediately.

'Right boys, what I'd like you to do, save standing in the cold, is leave your bikes over there – by the hedge – and come and sit in the car and we can deal with this in the warm.'

There was no possibility of getting away from this,

he thought, as he wheeled his bike to the side of the road. Michael was shaking off the brown rucksack stained dark and glistening wet.

'What's in the backpack then?' asked the policeman.

'A map, clothes and that. You know, we got a bit damp earlier on.'

'Better let me have a look then,' he said. 'Just to make sure.'

Two

Years before – two weeks ago – when he opened the back door he knew that his parents had been arguing. His mother was standing by the sink crossing Brussels sprouts. His father in the alcove, wearing his glasses and checking through bills. His sleeves pulled back to the elbow, wading through paper.

'Hello, dear,' said his mum, turning to smile. 'Did you have a good day?'

She had her hair tied back and a strand had come loose. It hung by the side of her face. She looked tired and rushed.

He went into the hall and dropped his school bag on the floor. He wondered what they were having for tea.

'Your mother asked you a question,' said his father, looking at him over the top of his glasses.

'Yes,' he said. 'What's for tea?'

'Cottage pie.'

He knew better than to point out that they'd had

cottage pie on Saturday. Today was Tuesday. He wondered if she'd forgotten. His father let out a loud sigh; he was busy checking a long list of entries. He always used a pencil for this. Pause. Tick. Pause. Tick. He stopped.

He said: 'We'll have to cut down on peak-time calls, Rebecca. You were on the phone to your mother for over an hour in February. We simply can't afford those kind of outgoings.'

His mother didn't say anything. She passed him a carrot.

'We're going on a field trip next week,' he said.

'Oh, really dear? Where to?'

He could tell that his father had stopped working and was listening to what he was saying.

'I've got a form in my bag. It's for Geography and Science. We're going to Helpston and some wildlife place.'

'I hope this isn't going to cost a great deal,' said his father. 'This will be the second time this term the school has asked for money.' He rubbed his eyes. 'I mean, this is supposed to be free education. We seem to be paying more and more each month – school trips – uniform – school fund. I've a good mind to phone that headteacher – ask her what's going on.'

His mother washed the sprouts and filled a saucepan

for the stove. She said quietly: 'It's not a lot, David. The theatre visit was eight pounds and I'm quite sure we can manage whatever it is that Tony needs now.'

'Just a packed lunch,' he said, 'and five pounds.'

His father sighed again – leaned on his elbow and resumed ticking.

Tony looked out of the kitchen window, out across the playing field at the centre of the estate. He could see the swings on Stratford Avenue. Someone was pushing the pirate ship. He could imagine the shrieking of the girls.

He went into the lounge and switched on the TV. A face came into view. It was screwed up, intense. A young woman snarling at someone not in the frame. She shouted: 'You said you were with Ben tonight, out at the country club. Well, Marie has just phoned to let me know that they can't come round tomorrow because Ben has been sick all day. So who were you with, Craig Holman, that's what I want to know.'

The camera cut to the face of a young man. His forehead was wrinkled with worry.

Just more hassle, Tony thought. Like school. He made the screen go blank.

When Mr Jordan talked about the field trip to Helpston he made it sound interesting – what with the wildfowl place and the nature reserve. He could tell that Michael thought so too. He'd stopped drawing boxes on the cover of his exercise book and listened.

Before Mr Jordan gave out the forms he said: 'Now class: we've got a full day organised for you and we'll be leaving from the car park at nine o'clock prompt. So as soon as you've been registered, come down and wait for the coach. I'll remind you of the exact procedure on Friday. If any of you think Mum or Dad might have difficulty with paying for the trip then they'll need to complete the slip at the bottom. We've got a special contingency fund for that sort of thing.'

He paused and looked round the room.

'Any questions?'

The trouble occurred in English. Mr Rolph had warned the class it was likely that they would be interrupted by an important visitor at some stage during the session.

'Just behave sensibly,' he said. 'Mr Carmell won't hurt you. If he asks you any questions, simply answer politely. And no you needn't stand up when he comes into the room.'

'Fat chance,' said Chris Phillips.

'So – so – and could you please stop tapping that pen, Paul Garnett? Yes? Thank you. Right class, I'd like

8

you all to get out your *Romeo and Juliet* stuff.'

There was a groan round the room.

'Why can't we ever do anything decent, sir?' said Melanie Brookes. 'I mean it used to be fun and interesting last year. You know, when we worked on the advertising project. That was really good, but this is dead boring.'

Michael grunted.

He put up his hand.

'Yes, Michael,' said Mr Rolph.

'Can't find my book,' he said.

'Can't find my book – what?'

'Can't find my book – well, that's it.'

'Will you please call me "sir" when you address me?' Mr Rolph's face had gone red.

'No need to get in a stress,' said Michael. 'Sir.'

'Well you'll just have to work on paper. There's a copy of the worksheet on the table.' He paused. 'Right. Everyone else got what they need?'

Tony opened his book. They had to draw the outline of a person and then write down all the ideas they had about Mercutio, one of the characters in the play.

'Want to come down the park later? After school?' asked Michael.

'Maybe,' he said. He thought of the Technology

project that needed to be finished. The revision for Friday's Maths test.

'What's this Mercutio or whatever's about then?' Michael said. 'What kind of name is that anyhow? Mercutio. Why can't they all have proper names – speak in English?' And then, looking in his bag, 'Here, lend's a pen.'

Tony gave him a ballpoint.

Michael chewed at the end, the scar on his top lip catching the light. Like a back-to-front 's'. Hooked from when his dad was still there, to take him fishing.

He looked down at Tony's copy of the play. 'Can't make head nor tail of all this stuff,' he said at last, and, half-turning, caught the table behind with his elbow.

'Michael Slater – you did that deliberately,' shouted Melanie. 'You've jogged my work. Sir – Mr Rolph – can you move this ape, sir – he's just ruined—'

'Who did you call an ape?' shouted Michael, standing up and pushing the table with his hand. Books, pens, pencils, rulers fell on to the floor.

'Come outside for a minute, Michael,' said Mr Rolph, pulling at his arm. 'Come on.'

'Out – out – out!' chanted Delaney and Squires from the back. 'Send him out!'

'And QUIET from the rest of you,' said Rolph. 'Get your books – open – and that includes you, Steven

Delaney. Right. Now, Michael Slater—'

But Michael had already taken advantage of the quiet in the classroom and was swaggering down the aisle, jogging the end table in passing.

'Sorr-ee,' he said as he opened the door.

The class fell silent when Mr Rolph went out. Everyone sat and tried to hear what was being said in the corridor.

He sat and tried to remember the nine-year-old who'd once said to him: 'You're new, aren't yuh? I'll show you around.'

After tea and when he'd finished drying up the plates, he said: 'I'm just going round the block. Shouldn't be long.'

His father called from the lounge: 'Do you have any homework?'

'A bit. Not much. It isn't for tomorrow, anyway.'

There was a pause and Tony wondered whether his father was going to appear and demand that he stayed at home and got his school stuff out. The bills by the bread bin were piled like storm clouds.

Once on his bike, he pulled away from the house and turned up towards Drayton Park, then along past the bowling green and the new houses.

When they had first come to Gretford from south

London, he used to go out at weekends cycling around the outside of the town. He often thought of it as a great island surrounded by green fields; a sea marked with stone villages and church spires. Over on the Stamford Road, on the opposite side, the fields were ridged into lines. You could see this really clearly whenever it snowed.

From their Year 5 History lessons he knew that these were the remains of an old way of farming, where everyone in the community had a strip of land and that was what they used for cultivation.

'In those days,' said Mrs Nightingale, 'few children in the villages went to school, and in fact most people weren't able to read or write. They would help their mums and dads and aunts and uncles work out in the fields.'

He remembered Michael Slater, who wasn't sitting next to him at that stage, saying: 'How do we get there, miss?' and everyone had laughed. But that was before the accident and before the sun dipped behind the clouds.

The pull up Weston Hill could be taken at a sprint now. He stood on his pedals and pushed down.

'It's like making the earth turn under your feet,' Michael had said on one of their expeditions into the countryside. 'Better'n sitting in a car and watching boring TV.'

From the top of the ridge, just before the avenue of lime trees, he paused and looked down over the town. From up here you could see the floodlights on the football ground and over to the left you could just make out the curved roof of the new cinema.

He could have called round and checked on Michael. Or picked up the phone and spoken to him. He wasn't around at the end of school and someone said that he'd been chucked out.

Michael was made to stay outside the classroom for five minutes by Mr Rolph, and when he came back he got on with the work quietly, using Tony's diagram for ideas, the ballpoint held in his large three-fingered grip. Where Tony had written 'friend' Michael had copied down 'frenid', like he couldn't see the way the letters were ordered.

At some stage, after Mr Rolph had told them to turn their notes into complete sentences, the door of the classroom opened and the headteacher, Mrs Stein, came in. She was followed by a large man in a blue pin-striped suit.

Everyone stopped working and looked up at the visitors.

'I'm sorry to disturb you, Mr Rolph – 9JR – but I'm

just showing Mr Carmell round and I thought he might be interested in seeing the work of an industrious English class.'

She looked out over the ranks of tables, smiling widely. She'd had highlights put in her hair, he noticed. Grey streaks against her natural brown. Eyes shining like polished glass.

'Quiet, class,' said Mr Rolph.

'This is Mr Carmell. He's a very important person. The chair of the school governors,' said Mrs Stein. She spoke slowly and clearly – as if to make sure they all understood. 'The governors are people from the community who meet every month to make sure that the school is running properly. Mr Carmell?'

'Hello,' he said. 'It's always a pleasure to get away from the office and drop into school. Just get on with your work and I'll come round and have a chat with you. Will that be all right, Mr Rolph?'

He reminded Tony of an army officer he'd once seen interviewed on TV. He'd been explaining how his men had been forced to take cover behind a wall because of enemy fire. He said 'sojers' when he meant 'soldiers'. Carmell was like that. He said 'Hullo' and 'orfice', and used 'all right' when he meant 'OK'. A voice like well-used leather.

The three of them stood at the front talking quietly

and he heard Mr Rolph explaining that this was a mixed-ability class.

'Youngsters of different talents? In the same class?' said Mr Carmell. His right eyebrow was raised.

'A policy that we're currently reviewing—' said Mrs Stein quickly.

Michael wrote: 'Murctio' and drew a line underneath it with Tony's pen. The pin-stripe was on the other side of the room chatting with Manvinder Tethi.

Michael looked down at his paper and at the diagram he'd copied from Tony.

'What do we do?' he said.

'Just – well,' said Tony, '– sort of turn the ideas into sentences. Like – you know – you are describing what he's like.'

'Was he the one in the film that was stabbed?' asked Michael. 'And took about forever to peg it?'

'Yeah.'

'Right. Gotcha.'

He bent over his paper. He quickly wrote: 'merctio was a frenid of romo he got into a fhigt with him and he was stabbd he took a long time to dhy.' He crossed out 'dhy' and wrote 'diy'.

'Hello?' said a deep voice, and Tony saw the large shadow next to them.

'How are you getting on?' He was speaking to

Michael. Mr Carmell had silver hair and a face that was blotchy and red. His teeth were uneven at the front, like some of the gravestones in the cemetery over at Weston.

'OK,' said Michael.

'What are you doing today?'

'Well, writing about this bloke in the play. The one who gets stabbed.'

He heard Melanie sniggering behind him.

He could smell onions and alcohol. Whenever Carmell spoke a great gust of stale air drifted across the table.

The pin-striped arm came across the page and a long forefinger touched the paper where Michael had written 'frenid'.

Carmell said, 'I don't think that's quite right. Can you see where you might change it?'

Michael looked down, his face turning red.

'Do you remember our old friend "i before e except after c"?' The hand reached across and pulled over Tony's book. He pointed to where Tony had written; 'Mercutio was a close friend of Romeo.'

'There,' said Mr Carmell, touching the word. 'Can you see how it goes?'

There was silence in the classroom. You could see the vein on Mr Rolph's forehead. He looked across the room to where they were sitting. He pulled at his ear lobe. Eyebrows drawn together.

'No, no I don't remember our "old friend", act-u-ally,' said Michael, pushing the table into the backs of the chairs in front, and standing up, 'and I don't want to.'

Mr Rolph had time to call, 'Michael Slater!' before Michael was through the door and pounding down the corridor, the fire door slamming back at the end.

'Time to review that – ah – "mixed ability" policy of yours, I think,' said Mr Carmell.

Three

Scratch Brook Community College
Northampton Road
Gretford Northants NN18 7RQ
Tel 03536 428731
Fax 03536 419043

Our ref: HW/RS/013
14 March

Dear Mrs Slater,
Michael ran out of school this afternoon after being
extremely rude to a visitor attending his English lesson.
This had followed an incident during the same lesson
when Michael had interfered with the work of another
student and had to be reprimanded by the class teacher,
Mr Rolph.

Although I appreciate that Michael doesn't always find the work easy, it's important that he learns to behave himself during school hours.

I would like to meet with you in the next week to discuss ways in which we can all work together to help Michael develop a more responsible attitude. Could you please contact the school and make an appointment with the office? I can be available any time after 3.30.

Until we've sorted this situation out I would ask you to keep Michael at home.

Yours sincerely,

Harriet Wilson
Head of Year

Four

'Going out to see Michael,' he called, zipping up his jacket and heading for the back door. His father in the dining-room; mother lost in TV.

'Just one moment,' his father answered. 'Just hold your horses.'

Tony waited, pulling his scarf tight against his neck.

His father appeared in the hall, a sheaf of papers in one hand, glasses in the other.

'Your mother has explained the situation with the Slater boy,' he said, coming into the kitchen. 'I appreciate that you've been a friend of his for years—'

'Dad, he's my oldest friend.'

'As I was saying, and as your mother has pointed out, Michael Slater has been in serious trouble at school before this. And quite honestly, Tony, I don't want you associating with that type of person.'

'But, Dad,' he said. 'Michael isn't a "type" of person. I mean, I know it looks bad but—'

'Looks bad isn't half of it. There was that incident when he assaulted another boy—'

'— after Delaney said his trainers were charity shop rejec—'

'— and now we've got this business where he's been rude to one of the governors.'

His mother came into the kitchen and ran the hot water.

His father said: 'Sometimes it's important to stand back and take a long, hard look at so-called friends.' Waving the papers in his left hand; signalling the end of the conversation. 'I'm sorry to have to speak to you so directly, but we need to take care of your best interests.'

His mother reached for the washing-up liquid from the box by the window.

Tony tugged his scarf loose. 'I think you're being unfair,' he said, to his father's retreating back. And then, louder: 'Totally unfair.'

Later, up in his room, he stood by his desk and looked out across the rooftops to the new industrial estate and the road that was completed last summer. Late sunlight bouncing off passing cars.

He pulled off the scruffy piece of A5 pinned to his noticeboard. It was written in pencil and was titled:

Finding fosils

The handwriting was small, with wide spacing – and there was an uncertainty about when capital letters should be used – so the total effect was of a field of weeds with a scattering of large, oversized thistles. Yet he knew the boy who had written the words had made a rough copy first, and then had carefully written up the account.

It was about Michael and himself. In Year 5. One hot lunchtime, when they'd crawled underneath one of the portable classrooms. In the cool dark, amongst the gravel, they'd found strange sea shells from long ago, and Mr King, the headteacher, said they were fossils.

'Like treasure,' Michael said, grinning.

And they'd stood up before the whole of Year 5 and spoken about their find, Mr King using an overhead projector to show everyone what fossils were. Their photographs were taken by the local paper.

'Michael Slater and Tony Hudson of Scratch Brook Primary', it said underneath – both of them smiling in the sun, their sweatshirts clean and their hands full of belemnites.

His finger touched the images, traced the faded picture, remembered the sunlight before the dreadful dark.

★ ★ ★

There was no sign of Michael when he cycled past his house those next afternoons after school. Once a light shone from his bedroom window, but there was no face at the glass; no waving hand; no figure turning circles on his bike over by the swings.

But then, as he stood with his backpack behind Chris Phillips, waiting to get on the coach for Helpston, there was a nudge in the ribs and a large smile breaking into 'Hiya!' as they moved forward and climbed the steps.

Later, after the old town had been swept away and they picked up the dual carriageway, Tony said: 'What did Miss Wilson have to say?'

Michael was silent for a moment or two.

'You know. Usual stuff about standards and everything. Crap about my dad. That kind of touch. Two weeks on a report card – you know, getting teachers to write what they think – every lesson. For two weeks. Yeah. And "good behaviour" for the rest of the year.' He smirked and then leaned across Tony and shouted at the tall, fair-haired boy on the opposite side. 'Here, Hargreaves – here, you tight git – give us one of those.'

Hargreaves was dipping his hand into his pocket and feeding himself with Prawn Delights.

'Get your own, Slater,' he said. 'When you've saved enough money.'

'Yeah, when my fist has helped you contribute.'

On the map, in class, the road went north-east in a straight line. It was coloured red and followed the valley of the Scratch Brook until the ruined Stanthorpe Abbey on the right-hand side.

Just after the Dunton roundabout there was a sudden roar and two jets came howling in low over the trees to their left, head down and streaking away beyond the reservoir at Wittering.

'Almost at Stamford,' he said to Michael who was looking out across the fields.

'Aye.'

'They'll be Harriers. Planes from the RAF station. I remember seeing the runways marked on the map.'

But his friend seemed to be in another place and so for the rest of the journey, to the wildfowl reserve, he'd studied the worksheet that Mr Jordan had handed out as they climbed on to the coach.

He was a new teacher – he couldn't have taken kids away before. Even Tony could see that you don't dish out worksheets before getting to the site. Half the class would have lost them by the time they got to Helpston and then what? Sharing? Miss Winthrop, from Science, wasn't much better. Built like a stick insect with teeth that jutted at the front. Always rabbiting on about being polite.

'That's a sandpiper,' said Mr Jordan, pointing towards a brown and white bird running along the edge of the pool on stilted legs. 'You'll notice the way it moves with head lowered and the tail – well,' he laughed, '– it bobs up and down almost continuously.'

'Right,' Tony said. Embarrassed. Wondering whether he should ask a question; knowing that if he did he'd get it in the neck from half the class.

'Saw you creeping up to Jordan. "What do they eat, Mr Jordan, sir?"' He could imagine it all now, with the orchestra of licking noises.

'Don't be frightened of being different, of standing out from the crowd,' his father had told him. 'Don't follow the herd like everyone else.' But it wasn't that easy, however interesting sandpipers might be.

And it was at that moment, just after Jordan had sloped off to annoy Susan Kitchener and Fiona Brickett, that he heard Michael's voice raised in fury: 'Don't do that, you git!' and the next moment Delaney was on the ground and Michael was standing over him, arms hanging loose, eyes like flint.

'Michael Slater – stop that at once,' shouted Mr Jordan, running across from the girls. Miss Winthrop appeared from a hide; two pensioners stopped to watch.

Steven Delaney slowly got to his feet, bent over, holding his ribs. His face was red when he looked at Michael. He said: 'You've made a mistake, Slater. You'll remember this.' He stabbed at Michael with his forefinger.

He bent to brush the mud from his trousers. 'I know where you live,' he said, spitting into the mud.

'Oh yeah – I'm trembling, Delaney.'

'Yes, all right, all right,' said Jordan. 'That's enough of the amateur dramatics. Both of you, come over here and let's get it sorted out.'

'That cretin was chucking stones at the ducks. Standing there and throwing bits of rock and stuff. Sorry if it's wrong and everything . . .'

'You liar!' said Delaney, grabbing Michael's jacket.

'Now stop it! Both of you!' Jordan separated them, and then, aware that everyone was staring at the two boys, turned to the class and shouted: 'Get ON with the questions on your sheets. We're leaving here in fifteen minutes. Now come over here. NOW!'

Tony stood looking out across the water. Colour was

returning to the trees and the bushes. There were light patches of white in the distance where the blackthorn was in flower. One of the earliest hedgerow blossoms, he remembered Michael saying. 'And completely vandal proof.'

'They're just stupid,' said Manvinder. 'Both of them.'

Mr Jordan was brandishing Michael's report card. He could hear bits of the conversation that mingled in with the noises of the waterfowl.

'. . . absolute disgrace that you should behave . . . when we get back I shall be discussing this with your form teacher . . . coming here and throwing stones at the wild birds . . .' on and on and on. Some of the phrases, some of the expressions he'd heard before. Like they were the words that all teachers used when they got angry. When he was younger he'd wondered whether there wasn't some special book – like a phrase book or something – that was given to new teachers. So that they could pick up the standard terms of abuse.

At Helpston they got out to look at the church and answer questions on the construction of the old cottages. There were flowers in some of the windows and posters advertising an election. They said: VOTE HAYDON JONES or VOTE SAMUEL

JENKINS. Blue on white; yellow on red. Like football teams, he thought. Support your side! Leicester for the Cup!

On the coach south to Ailsworth Heath, Michael was made to sit at the front with Mr Jordan. Steven Delaney was seated next to Miss Winthrop. Michael sat slumped, hands in his pockets, unseeing as the road unwound.

'We'll be here for forty minutes, students,' said Mr Jordan when the coach had stopped. 'This is a bit of wild heathland which dates back at least one thousand years. There's a picnic area ahead of us with benches and tables and you'll find that there's a stream and pool through the trees ahead. The ground beyond the trees is quite boggy so I wouldn't recommend any of you wandering too far away. And I don't want to see anyone messing around. We've had enough upsets for one day.'

He turned to Michael and Steven Delaney. 'Right, you two. Have your lunch. Keep away from each other. Is that understood?'

They both grunted.

'Let's go and have a look at the water,' said Michael as soon as they were off the coach.

'But I thought Jordan—'

'He didn't say we couldn't. Just some cack about

messing about. And we're not messing about – just finding out.' He laughed.

There was a track beneath a huddle of silver birch, a rickety wooden gate and then a large pool opened in front of them, reeds on the far side, the grass beneath their feet soft and wet. Water like polished steel.

They walked carefully on the ridges of tyre tracks, following the path that was quickly turning to mud. There were trees to their right and strands of barbed wire that fenced off some new development. Where the pond began to curve round to the left, they stopped and scanned the surface, their eyes checking for fish.

'Look down there,' said Michael, pointing. 'There, do you see? There's a – in fact there's two – sort of worm-like things – five centimetres long – can you see?'

There were two pale strands, like thickened spaghetti. They seemed to be anchored to the bottom of the pond and swayed back and forth in the slight current. Freshwater anemones.

'Yeah,' he said. 'What are they then?'

'Leeches,' said Michael.

'You mean—'

'Yeah – primitive, bloodsuckers. The vampires of the pond world.'

'Where do you get all this stuff, Michael?'

'I – dunno.'

They looked across at the trees on the other side, and in the silence Tony could hear the distant splashing of trickling water. Like a bath being filled two floors away. In another place he knew he'd tripped into Michael's past.

'Dad.'

A blackbird left its perch and disappeared into the thicket behind them.

Michael bent down and pulled at a grass stalk.

'Left me some books – with big pictures. When I was a kid we used to go out on his motorbike. Fishing and that. You get to know a bit about the countryside. How it works.'

He listened to these old memories, watching Michael, as he groped and stumbled across this other world.

Later, they returned to the track. Among the trees primroses starred the bank and at one point, close to, they heard the screech of a pheasant, like metal being ripped. Where a stream entered the pool, they sat on an earth bank and looked over at where the coach was parked. It was out of sight and they couldn't hear the chatter of the others.

'Stuffing their faces,' Tony said.

'Yeah.' Michael leaned forward and ran his hands

through the water, stopped, and said: 'What's that – over there?'

To begin with he couldn't make anything out in the shadows thrown by the trees, but then, his eyes following Michael's arm, he saw a black shape take form in the grey.

Michael looked round.

'What we need is a bit of stick. Something like that.' He stood up and went into the undergrowth. 'Come on, give us a hand. No. This'll do. Probably a bit of hazel. Feels rotten.' He struggled to free the branch from the tangle of weeds and ground ivy. And later, like a cartoon angler, he was bent over the water, the branch stretched out, prodding below the surface.

'It's not that deep,' Michael said. 'With wellies we could – probably – wade out and pick it up – but, ah, wait a minute. There's definitely some – thing. Yes.'

They both stared at where the branch disappeared and then, easing back and up, a dark mass of mud and weed came clear of the surface, dribbling water, flashing silver.

'It's really – quite – difficult.'

'You don't think it's just a—'

'Can of worms?' said another voice, and the next moment they were shoved forward, water rising to meet their fall, hands sinking into the silt, mouths filled with the taste of old earth and dead leaves.

A moorhen flapped away and they had just time to turn and see the blade-thin smile of Steven Delaney.

'Nice trip,' he shouted. 'I'll tell Jordan about your fight.'

And with that he disappeared into the wood.

Five

Waht hapned
I was with tnoye husdon we wher geting som thing out of the
pond we wer useing a stik from the wode I had got the jar out
of the pond but we wher pused in tow it thats how we got wet

Michael Slater

Six

He woke up to hear his parents arguing. His father shouting at his mother. It was 7.18.

'Did you know anything about this? Did you have any idea of what he'd been up to? You must have noticed that his clothes were filthy? Did he explain what had happened?'

'Look, David, I'm quite sure there's a simple explanation for all this. The school has probably got the wrong end of the stick. And as for his clothes – well – I haven't emptied his laundry basket yet so—'

'So he's hidden the evidence? We'll see about that!' and with that there was the sound of his father's feet on the stairs, pounding up to where he lay, his eyes closed in the darkness.

'And you can stop that pretence,' said his father, switching on the light and going over to his laundry basket. He picked it up, grabbed the top – and emptied the contents across his bed. The trousers and sweatshirt,

34

crumpled and muddy, tumbled out with the rest.

'So exactly how do you account for this?' he said. 'Trying to hide the fact that you were involved in a fight whilst out on a field trip? Fighting with the Slater boy? Shaming yourself and your family? What in heaven's name do you think you were up to? Did you think it was clever to push your so-called friend into a pond? And what was the outcome of all this?' His father reached into his jacket pocket and produced the letter from the school.

'"As a result of their wet condition,"' he read, '"and because of their behaviour it was decided to cut short the Year 9 trip.

'"This was very unfortunate for everyone concerned and resulted in great disappointment to those students who behaved responsibly. We have refunded 50% of the cost of the trip to all the parents of the students affected by the behaviour of the minority.

'"We feel you should discuss the matter with Tony. We have placed him on report for the next two weeks and we would like you to sign his card each evening. This will enable you to check on his progress and in particular, his behaviour.

'"This is the first time I have had to write to you respecting your son's conduct and I find it regrettable that I should have to do so now. I feel confident that there will be no repetition."'

'Too right there won't be a repetition. You'll stay in for the next month. You'll show me your homework each and every night and finally, I do not wish you to associate with the Slater boy. That's not just for the next week or month, it's for good. I shall write to . . .' he looked at the name at the bottom of the letter, 'to Miss Wilson and make our feelings known.'

And with that he was out of the door and stamping down the stairs.

Maybe it was the result of the morning's trouble with Michael and Delaney, but by the time they had got back to the coach, and after the great burst of laughter had subsided from the rest of the class, Mr Jordan had made it clear that he wasn't in any mood for excuses. Or explanations. Certainly not of the 'It wasn't our fault' variety.

'I don't want to hear your lies,' he had said, eyebrows drawn together, tie hanging off-centre. 'I'm absolutely sick to death of your behaviour, Slater. You've been a pain in the backside ever since we set off this morning. And now this.' He paused, and then; 'As for you, Tony Hudson, I'm amazed – absolutely amazed – that you should get yourself involved. Exactly what did you think you'd get out of this?'

'Water wings,' shouted someone from the class.

'Be quiet,' snapped Miss Winthrop, turning to scowl at the boys.

'I've discussed this with Miss Winthrop and we've decided that there's no alternative but to cut short the trip and return to school. We cannot possibly carry on with the pair of you wandering around completely soaked to the skin.'

'That's not fair,' said Melanie Brookes. 'We don't deserve to suffer because of those two idiots.'

'Yeah,' said Delaney. 'Idiots.'

The three-mile ride home turned into a marathon that night. He cut up through the Scratch Brook estate, past the chattering groups of children and women with pushchairs.

He didn't bother with the path across the water meadow, but struck out along the ridge, towards Hannington. Delaying the inevitable.

Michael had been sitting outside Mrs Stein's office at the end of school. He had smiled and raised his hand as Tony figured out something to say. He knew better than to go and have a chat to his friend. The raised hand and thin smile, what did that mean: 'Hi!'? 'I'll see you!'?

And how was he going to explain to Mum,

and, more seriously, to his father, exactly what had happened?

At the time, sitting in the Head of Year's office, he'd felt ashamed. Like he had committed a criminal offence. It was like it had happened to someone else. Not the person who'd crawled beneath the temporary classroom and made the great fossil discovery. Working with Michael to sort out the assembly. The two boys with their pictures in the paper.

He wanted to be able to get his old self back, not get caught up in this thing that was out of his control. He hadn't spoken when Miss Wilson had said, 'Have you anything to say?' because he felt the disappointment on her face, in her eyes, and he realised that if he tried to explain what had happened, if he said they hadn't been doing anything wrong, simply trying to get an old can or whatever out of the water, well, he'd start crying. It was like everything he'd done at school was wiped out by this single act of '. . . thoughtlessness' and he realised that she had simply carried on talking.

Did Michael ever feel like this? Even at the beginning when he'd first been shouted at? Given that first detention? Made to stand up in front of the class and explain why he had tripped somebody up?

But Michael was different. In fact Michael had changed in some way. There seemed to be an anger about him sometimes, as if he *enjoyed* arguing with teachers.

He clicked up a gear. Ahead a rabbit dropped from the verge into the hedgerow as he turned into the dog-leg at Hannington. It was pale brown, its white backside like a streak of paint.

Michael seemed to take trouble in his stride.

Down the slope and into the village. He pushed into third. There was the usual gaggle of ducks by the stream and a toddler feeding them from a bag. Her mum was saying: 'That's it. Throw the bread at the birds. Throw the bread, Jemima.'

For everyone else life seemed to carry on as normal. Mums and toddlers went to feed ducks; his dad carried on with his business; rabbits nibbled at grass on verges. But for him, it was like he'd changed places with someone else – had been given a new face. He felt strange and adrift.

He turned left after the village, the road gradually dropping down by the estate wall. Crichton House soon came into view over his left shoulder. Someone had told him it was designed like a French château. He wouldn't know. He'd never been inside. Michael's dad had worked there. He was an under-manager.

If Michael had changed, he thought, it was since that time his dad had failed to come home from work. The night when he'd heard the ambulance belting past their house, the blue light flashing on to the dining-room wall. And then the empty place next morning when Miss Thorn had taken the register. She hadn't even paused to say, 'Michael Slater? No? Anyone seen Michael today?', like she knew what had happened.

As he cycled through the park, the first lights appearing on Windsor, he tried to figure out what to say when he opened the door and went into the kitchen, his clothes still damp from the trip. Because he wondered if Miss Wilson might have lifted the phone at school and explained what had happened. And he wondered also, whether he should tell his parents that it wasn't his fault, and that Michael wasn't to blame.

But when he opened the back door, his mother looked up from her paper and said: 'Did you have a good time, dear?' and he simply slipped away from her mild gaze and stuffed his trousers and sweatshirt into his laundry basket.

'What did you do?' she asked when he came down.

'Michael Slater spotted these worm-like things. In a pond over on this heathland. They were leeches.'

'Really?' She paused from putting cans in the cupboard. 'I thought you only got leeches in hot countries?'

'No. He says not.'

'Tony . . .' She closed the cupboard door and came over to the table. 'About Michael Slater.'

'Yeah.'

'I don't mean to go on.' She had looked pained, her mouth pulled into a line. She went over to the sink. 'I think you should be seeing less of him. I mean—'

'Has Dad told you to say that?'

She removed the lid from the kettle, turned the cold tap.

'Don't be rude, Tony. He does have a point you know.'

'Mum, when we first came here, Michael was the lad who came and showed me around. You said he was OK then – it was nice for me to make friends so quickly.'

'Things have happened in Michael's life that none of us can be blamed for and – well – we're – your dad and I, we're concerned that you'll get yourself into trouble if you carry on like this.'

'Right. OK.'

He went up to his room and sat at his modelling desk. He looked down at the nearly completed Bristol Bulldog. The silver paint hadn't streaked this time and you could see the detail of the ribs on the upper surface of the wings, imagine the canvas stretched over the frame. Yet why were the ailerons positioned at the front of the wings, he wondered, turning the plane into the light. Was this some kind of experimental design? But wouldn't such an arrangement badly affect the balance of the aircraft? Make handling difficult? The airflow would be interrupted and surely this would make the plane highly unstable?

He looked at the plan from the set of instructions in the box. The wings were the wrong way round! It was simply a matter of using the craft knife to unhinge the wings from the struts and then reattach them correctly.

He held the Bulldog with his thumb and forefinger, just behind the cockpit, moving it so that it appeared to be flying straight into his face, imagining the noise, the wind, the smell of oil and kerosene. Things might actually look OK on the outside but be useless when you really thought about it. And vice versa.

He wondered when the letter from Miss Wilson would arrive at their house. And he wondered what he would say when it did.

His father arrived early for tea. He heard the front door slam and then the sudden burst of noise from the opened kitchen door. The radio news blasting up the stairs to where he sat.

There was a sharp click, silence, and then his father

said: 'I think we may have to close the magazine, Rebecca. We can't afford losses on this scale.'

Seven

He lay on his bed. Looking up at his planes. They were all headed due south. Like a cluster of migrating birds, beating away from the cold. Out of trouble. Straight and level.

In the space under his bedside table, on top of the stack of *Computer Monthly*, there was a copy of his dad's magazine, *Break Away*. 'Free Tickets for Bedford Zoo!' it said on the cover, beneath the picture of the chimp sitting in the fork of a tree.

Turn the pages and you'd find holiday information about what to do and where to go with your young family. Want to ride on a steam train? – Three to choose from. Fancy wandering around a working farm? Spend a day at a theme park? Discover the secrets of the past? Every family taste catered for, it seemed. With five pages of diary events to take you safely through to the next half-term.

Downstairs, in the kitchen, he knew his father would

be sitting at the table and his mother standing with her back against the draining board, listening. He would look down into his hands, and then turn to explain himself to her, his face twisted as though he were in some kind of pain. He was saying: 'We're going to take a hammering with this issue.'

Tony stood by his bedroom door, head bent in concentration.

'About two and a half grand down at the moment – that's if the phone bill doesn't go through the roof.'

His voice got louder and Tony knew that he would have got up and would be walking round the kitchen, thinking and talking.

'We've had three cancellations today, including Big Sea,' he said. 'Completely out of the blue.'

Tony sat down. He reached for the magazine. When you turned the front cover and looked at the page facing you, there was a black box at the bottom. It said:

ADVERTISING

Break Away appears six times a year and is distributed free to the families of children in primary schools.

> Our aim is to help parents find interesting attractions for their children when they're out of school.
>
> If you would like to advertise a service with us please phone 03536 382718 and we will explain our rates and conditions.
>
> We operate an inexpensive design studio for customers who need help with layout.

Twenty-two months of late nights and early starts and *Break Away* was teetering on the edge of the chasm posted 'closure'. Advertisers were nervous to begin with, he remembered. Constantly grumbling about the service they received. Complaining ads were not in the right place; colours too weak; size wasn't what they'd ordered.

It certainly wasn't what they'd imagined when his father had arrived home that December with the news of this great idea and that at long last he'd be able to tell Thompson's Shoes exactly what they could do with their new Wild Life range.

Because the magazine was 'a perfect example of focused marketing'.

But then – cancelled adverts, unpaid bills, problems

with the office computer – the list went on and on. In twenty-two months the world became unreasonable, unmanageable. And everything got on his father's nerves: the way Tony ate his cereal, the time he spent watching television, the money he needed to go to the pictures or even to buy a pair of football boots.

'But he's got to have them,' he remembered his mother saying, her face grey and tired in the steam of the kitchen.

So it wasn't a great surprise, he thought as he clicked the gears up a notch and pedalled away from the house, that his father'd go over the top about the letter from Miss Wilson. Tony felt the school report card in his coat pocket. Like a letter he had to post.

He waited for the stream of cars to pass him on the Scotton Road before turning into Windsor. Clicking down and pulling in to allow a car to pass on the other side.

Above the DIY store a dove sat coo-cooing, its voice magnified against the walls of the houses, its collared head turning to look at its mate on the ridge. *Coo-coo*, they said, back and forth. *Coo-coo*.

He focused his mind on the card; filed *Break Away* in the place marked 'Later'.

After all, it wasn't the reaction of other kids that

bothered him about the card: there was a kind of respect and curiosity that attached itself to being 'on report'. No, he'd quite like that side of things, the celebrity; the problem was how to get back to where he had been; how to find a place at school where he could simply get on with the things that he liked. And where people liked him.

He clicked down through the gears, standing up to press speed from the back wheel, and at the top of the hill almost rode straight into Michael Slater, sitting astride his mountain bike at the entrance to the park.

Michael said: 'We'll have to go back. You know that, don't you?'

He wore his faded blue sweatshirt and jeans. Hair hanging in front of his eyes, a cut on his lower lip.

What did he mean?

Tony checked his watch.

'It's OK,' said Michael. 'You've got plenty of time.' He laughed and spat.

'What happened to you yesterday, when we got back?'

'Chucked out, mate, twice in two weeks. Some kind of record I shouldn't wonder.' There was a pause and Tony could hear the rustling of starlings above.

'How – like – how serious is it?' he asked, thinking,

is this the end? Will Michael be expelled? Made to go to another school?

Michael shrugged. 'Got to go in front of the beak – a governor – next Monday evening. With Mum and everything.' He leaned on his handlebars. He turned his head: 'Been there before, Tony. Just a load of cack.'

'So – so – what're you doing?'

'Waiting for you, that's what. Anyway,' – he sat back on his saddle – 'we've got unfinished business. Stuff to do – back at the heath. Like I said, we've got to go back.'

'What d'you mean?'

'You know.' He looked at Tony, his eyes grey and direct. 'Got to find that mug or jug or whatever. It's gonna be worth a bob or two. Sure of that.'

'Yeah – but – you know – it could simply be an old can or something. People chuck loads of things in places like that. Could have been someone having a picnic.'

'I don't think so. What you didn't see – and I don't blame you because the next thing we were up to our faces in mud – was that I'd caught it by a handle. I think it's something to drink from. Metal. I mean,' – and he spread his arms out, smiling – 'even you must see it's worth going back, fishing it out – having a look.'

He was grinning broadly, thumbing the gears back and forth.

'It's thirty miles, Michael. *At least.* There isn't a bus from here and the old man wouldn't think about driving us. He's sorting out the magazine. You know?'

Michael looked around. He said: 'We'll bike it, mate. Take the yellow roads. The ones on the maps at school. We've got – you've got – Geography this p.m. See if you can, hem, "borrow" one. That dozy git Jordan doesn't know the time of day. I'll wait for you at the barn – after the Hannington turn-off. Enjoy school!'

'Enjoy school', he thought, his head full of Michael's off-the-wall suggestion. First the report card, then this. His father's face in close-up: 'Looking after your best interests,' he'd said. And then Miss Wilson, disappointment tugging at the corners of her mouth: 'Think what you're doing – use your brain.'

There was more *Romeo and Juliet* in English; a demonstration of a van de Graaff generator in Science with Miss Winthrop ('It'll make your hair stand on end,' she said, smiling out of her yellow sweater).

And then Mr Jordan. Geography. Ribbon development and the industrial revolution.

He went to Jordan's desk at the start of the lesson, after everyone else had filed in, and placed his barely crumpled report card next to the heap of exercise books. Looked down at the thinning hair of the teacher. A glance up and then: 'Ah, Tony, I'm sure you'll be off this in no time.'

The Ordnance Survey maps were piled neatly at the back of the room, next to the blue Stones atlases, by the window. Every now and then he would turn and look at them, once catching the eye of Steven Delaney who sneered and raised his middle finger.

And you, he thought.

At one point, on the excuse of borrowing a ruler, he went over to Chris Phillips, his hand reaching out to the stack.

'Hurry up, Tony, you're blocking the light,' said Mr Jordan.

And so he went back to his seat, underlining the title, Rural Communities.

As he wrote about the way villages developed, about their location and expansion, so he thought about the meeting with Michael, about the events at Ailsworth Heath and about the report card lying at the front of the class, on Jordan's desk.

And he wondered, as he sat answering the questions Mr Jordan wrote on the board, whether he wasn't just a little frightened of Michael Slater and what he might do, and so, when the bell rang and while he waited for Jordan to write a comment on his card, he said: 'Can I borrow one of the maps? One of the maps that contains Ailsworth Heath?'

Jordan stopped writing, in fact had got as far as 'Excell—', and stared at Tony as if the other had confessed to armed robbery. 'You want to borrow an OS map, Tony?'

'Yes, sir,' conscious of the Year 7s outside in the corridor; faces peering in through the glass in the door.

'A bit of private research, Tony?' asked Jordan, his eyebrows raised.

'Yeah – sort of. I'd look after it. Only need it for a couple of days.'

'Hmmm. OK,' said the teacher, getting up and going to the back of the room. 'Here you are. Look after it. They're about a fiver a shot these days. You can have it until Monday.'

'Thanks.' He went to the door.

'Oh, and Tony?'

'Yes?' he said, his hand pulling the door half-open.

'I don't blame you for the problem we had yesterday. But, well, you need to choose your friends – ah – carefully.'

'Ye-es' he said. 'Yes.' And then he was through the mass of eleven-year-olds and running down the corridor. He could hear Jordan behind him, his voice shouting out instructions: 'A disgraceful noise. You can jolly well all line up again. Without talking, Nigel May. Yes, you.'

By the time he got to Drama, the others had gone into the studio and were sat listening to Mrs Kaur outlining the lesson. Stewart Green made a space for him in the circle.

Michael's blue mountain bike was slung on the ground behind the hawthorn hedge in front of the barn on the Hannington road. Michael was sitting on a stack of bales, a piece of straw in his mouth.

'You took your time,' he called.

'Had to see Wilson. About the card.'

'Right. I forgot.' He climbed down into the mud. 'Get the map, then?'

Tony opened his backpack. 'Yeah. But look after it. I borrowed it. Until Monday.'

'You what?' Michael stopped in the act of unfolding the sheet. 'Borrowed it? You mean you actually asked Jordan, that slug, if you could borrow the map? — "Please, Mr Jordan sir, slurp, would you mind ever so much if I took one of your delightful maps home? Just for the weekend, sir?"' His mouth moved cartoon-like, large, exaggerated, the syllables being pushed and pulled. It was grotesque.

He was silent, feeling the anger mount in his chest.

'I got the map, Michael. Why should it matter how? You tell me that.'

'Well, mate,' he replied, 'let's get a couple of things sorted: as a result of your Mr Jordan, I've been booted out of school. Maybe permanently.' He paused. 'It's not like – like – I can run off home and get the old man to drive up to Scratch Brook and tell Mrs Hitler a thing or two about how she runs her school. And why's that I wonder? Because when I goes home to see Mummy, she says: "Now what have you done, Michael, you'll be the death of me."'

He stopped talking and they were both silent. Where they stood, where the grass was worn away into earth and dried mud, there were the footprints of cattle. The light wind rattled the corrugated metal of the barn. A lorry jolted past.

'Let's look at the map shall we?' Tony said.

Eight

One summer, when he'd first come to Gretford, and shortly after he'd met Michael, they'd been caught by an afternoon thunderstorm. Over at Weston Park, by the stream and among the swings.

The other kids – Robert Gould and Amardeep Lall – had legged it at the first crack of thunder, but Tony and Michael wheeled their bikes and stuck it out beneath a tree. Watching the rain pattern the circle of dust beyond the trunk.

At some stage, as the sky began to lighten and the storm hitched a ride in another direction, they'd both noticed this great scarf of colour curving away above the trees on the ridge.

And Tony'd said: 'Hey, wouldn't it be great – really great – to be able to stand in a rainbow – at the place where the colours land on the ground. You'd – well – you'd see the world differently. You'd move your head and there'd be red clouds or blue grass.'

And Michael, looking at the rainbow, had said, 'Yeah, let's do it,' and turned his handlebars and was splashing to the gate without further discussion.

They'd hit the road and ploughed up as if it was on the flat and chased each other down the lane, on and on, red-faced and sweating. And fetched up? Amongst the cow parsley and nettles and stink of a sewage farm: great concrete cylinders and a sign that said KEEP OUT.

He thought of that moment, where they'd stood panting and wet and deceived, as he unfolded the map, spread it out on top of the bale stack. Like planning another stupid adventure, he thought. Like kids.

'Look,' said Michael, a dirty fingernail picking up the yellow road stretching east out of Gretford through Weston and Hannington and then down the hill into Calderhay. 'That's the road, there – right?' looking at Tony for confirmation. 'So we need to cross this red 'un—'

'Yeah,' said Tony, noting the blotches of green, the dribbles of blue, the great curves of the main roads cutting the landscape.

'Whatever – and then – where's Oundle on this sheet?'

Tony pointed.

'Right. So we follow the yellow 'un as far as Oundle and then we should be able to find the Nene Way which will take us past the water meadows, through the town and—'

'Nope,' Tony said suddenly. 'Nene way's useless. We'd end up carrying the bikes through a load of quag.'

He surprised himself with his sudden interest in the crazed idea. Looked at like this, sitting four metres above the field, with the map spread between them, it was like they were working out the escape route from some prisoner of war camp. A scene from one of the old black-and-white films his father occasionally watched on slow Sunday afternoons. Kid's stuff then.

'Stick to the side road there.' He pointed. 'See – Fotheringhay and Wansford.' Where the A1 was curled into a knot.

'– And so, to the heath – and to the secret of the pool!' Michael looked up, grinning. 'Come on, mate,' he said, 'even a boring old fart like you must find this exciting?' He punched his arm lightly.

'You're crazy, Michael. We couldn't – not in one day. Not even with a wind behind us. It's . . .' He paused, looking down at the veins and arteries and ribbons of colour that crossed the sheet between them. '. . . It's got to be thirty miles. At least. To Ailsworth. Could be forty because of the small roads—'

'Start early,' said Michael. 'Leave at seven. Even if it's forty, I bet we'd be there by one. And that would be—'

'Six hours – we'd have to do a shade over five miles an hour to get there – and the traffic, past the A1 – you know what it's like.' He thought of the lorries and rented vans that so often pushed him into the kerb; the cars that cut in front, that made sudden turns.

'You worry too much,' said Michael. He laughed. 'Anyway, five miles an hour? No problem, you know that.'

'The other thing . . .' He paused, trying to find the correct form of words. 'I'm grounded for the next month.'

'What not allowed out after school? No weekends?'

Tony looked down. He said: 'Yeah, that's about the size of it.'

'Well, that's two of us, mate. I thought the old dear was going to take a stroke when she got the latest letter from school.'

'It's not only that, but – I – well—'

'Spit it out, why don't you?' Michael struggled with the creases of the map.

'The old man doesn't want me to hang around with you.' He rubbed the side of his nose, not meeting the gaze of the other.

'Bad influence, eh?' said Michael, punching his arm

58

and grinning. 'Not good enough to be your friend? So,' – he hurled the map into space – 'we'll go Friday. Get everything sorted tomorrow and you can have an early holiday the day after. Join me on the great north ride!'

It was a second or two before he realised what Michael was suggesting and a second or two more to work out what to say.

'I'll think about it,' he said.

'Don't get your knickers in a whatsit,' said Michael. 'Piece of cake. Done it loads and loads of times. Never been caught yet. Well, only once – but that was an accident.' He grinned.

'What do you mean?'

'Duh. Registers are marked with pencils, right? Teachers use different codes. Go into school late Friday. Get there a shade after nine o'clock. All the registers will have been returned and classes will be in assembly or having form periods. Take the register from the shelf, rub out the absent mark and pencil in a straight line. Shows you're there. Over the afternoon slot, pencil in a "P" – means that the office has received a phone call from a mum – saying you're ill. It also means,' he said, standing up and stretching, 'it also means, you don't have to bring a note on Monday because of the phone call on Friday.'

He was silent. The air smelt of old straw and cattle.

There were rooks wandering over the field opposite, stabbing the earth.

'I don't know,' he said. 'I'll call you.'

'Phone's off at the moment,' said Michael. 'Better meet here. After school.'

Later, when he'd dried up the tea things, his father called him into the dining-room. Where the PC was kept, the filing cabinet and files stuffed with paper; the noticeboard with its chart of dates in bold black pen.

His father had changed into a white polo-necked sweater, his wavy brown hair newly combed, his broad hands smelling of soap.

'Have you got your report card, Tony?' he asked, looking across the table.

'Yes.' He passed it over.

'Mmm. Good in English and Science; excellent in Geography and Drama. So,' his father smiled, eyes magnified by the lenses, 'it's not all doom and gloom then? You can do some things right.'

Silence. He was expected to speak. He said: 'Yes.'

'What's the homework situation? What have you got tonight?' He handed the report card back.

'Have to finish writing up notes for English. For Friday. Revision for a Maths test.'

'Right.' His father took his glasses off, rubbed his eyes.

'Sorry to have to go through this procedure, Tony. But after what's happened I think it's vital that we establish some sense of structure. To help you with your work at school.' Pause. 'Do you understand what I'm saying?'

'Yes.'

'Been keeping out of Slater's way?'

'He's suspended, Dad.'

'Right. Well, that's what comes when you play fast and loose with the regulations. Look, come and show me how you've got on this evening. When you've finished the work.'

'Yes,' and then he'd turned and left his father with his files and spreadsheets and letters and floppy disks of data.

The phone went a little after seven. He stopped writing about the character of Romeo and turned to listen. His mother called from the hall. She said: 'David? It's for you. Someone from Long View Finance.'

There was a pause, then he heard the door of the dining-room open. His father picked up the receiver.

'Hello yes, this is David Hudson speaking. Right, right, Mr Mayhew, I am aware of the situation . . . Yes

. . . Yes . . . I appreciate what you're saying, but if you . . . if you could just listen to . . . Look I spoke to Mr Grayson only yesterday morning. The position is that yes, we do have a cash-flow problem at the moment and I know we are two months behind with the payments, but I should be able to settle the backlog in the next week. I'm chasing our creditors at the moment. Yes . . . I appreciate that. OK. Yes. I understand. Obviously . . . That would be very drastic and we . . . look we don't envisage getting into a situation like that. Of course . . . well, thank you for calling. Goodbye.'

And he replaced the receiver. Went into the lounge. In the distance his mum said: 'What did they want?'

Silence and then: 'The house,' his father replied. 'We've got four weeks to raise six thousand pounds.'

Nine

'Before I hand out the certificates, I want to talk to you about success.'

Mr Carmell, centre stage, dark suit, silver hair, standing to one side of the lectern. He cleared his throat. Tony remembered the stale breath, the hand on the page. The Chair of Governors.

'It seems to me that success isn't just about scoring goals for Manchester United. Nor is it about getting a number one record in the hit parade. These things are a kind of success and we all know about them – but they're simply the glitzy, glamorous images we see on our televisions or read about in our newspapers.

'What I mean by success are those things all of us can achieve. Everyone, whatever their situation, can attain.'

Tony studied the back of Daniel Croft's neck. Noticed the dandruff on the shoulders of his sweatshirt. Like dust, he thought.

'Success is about overcoming difficulty and often overcoming resistance within ourselves. The youngster who suddenly decides to get up early and make his bed instead of relying on Mum to do it for him – well he's making great strides in becoming a mature adult.

'The youngster who gets home from school and helps Mum get the tea ready or who starts to do the washing up when the tea has been eaten – well that's success as well, isn't it? The ability to decide to change the environment in some way – to make things better for other people.

'And everyone can achieve some measure of success in their lives each and every day. However difficult circumstances can seem, there's always something that can be done.'

One of the strip lights in the ceiling was flickering. It seemed to be switched off but every few seconds it flashed into life and then went out. Like the programme on pulsars he'd seen: stars spinning in a dance of death.

'We're gathered here to celebrate a number of students who have made great changes in their lives and who have proved to be a credit to themselves, to their parents – and to the staff of this school.

'And we are all proud of them. Proud that their

attendance has been so high. That their work has been so good. That they've achieved so well in a variety of public examinations. They are examples to us all.'

Pause.

Someone started clapping at the back and then everyone in the hall joined in. The teachers at the side, the rows of students around Tony, the senior staff on the stage behind Mr Carmell.

Clap clap clap.

A pied wagtail ran across the paving outside.

Clap clap clap.

He watched a crisp packet scrape across the ground by the dustbins. He thought of the phone call he'd overheard.

He didn't clap.

His mother had said: 'How much are we owed, David?'

'A shade over four, maybe four and a half thousand. But you know, Rebecca,' – and he could imagine his father's outstretched arms, as if appealing to his wife for agreement – 'you know that we've been chasing these creditors, we've been chasing everyone who owes us more than fifty pence. I mean,' and his voice grew fainter, 'it's not as though we've let grass grow under our feet.'

'I know that, David,' and he could tell that his mother

had got up to comfort him. 'You've gone through the county court every time.'

'Now I'd like to hand out silver certificates for those students who have achieved eighty commendations in the last term.'

Mrs Stein had stood up and was referring to a list. She said: 'I think it will make the show run a bit more smoothly if we applaud everyone at the end.' A flash of white teeth. 'Mary Bridges, Anita Chauda, Baljinder Kaur, Stuart Leeson, Wesley Morgan . . .'

His mother was saying: 'We're not dead yet you know. I can ask Mrs Prentice if I can extend my hours.'

Outside he heard a blackbird begin its excited chatter. Standing on a branch of the pear tree. If he looked down there'd be a cat slinking across the lawn.

His father said: 'We're talking six grand, Rebecca. And four weeks. A few more hours as a classroom assistant won't dent that.'

'What about the bank?'

'We owe them eight thousand from the original loan.'

Another bird joined from next door's garden. A general alert then.

Later, he'd put his school stuff in his bag and got changed for bed. He lay for some time looking up at the planes flying across his ceiling, trying to get his thoughts to drift away from that strange expression his father had used.

He'd said they'd 'wanted the house'. The credit company. What did that mean? If he didn't pay them all the money that was owed would they have to give them the house instead? But how could that be, if they paid a mortgage to the bank? Surely the bank wouldn't allow that to happen?

He woke up in the night to hear his mother and father talking. His mother was saying: 'Everything looks black at this time of night, David. Try and get some sleep.'

And he lay awake until he saw the first touches of grey appear beneath his curtain and the first birds started to sing.

After the celebration assembly he realised he'd packed his bag for the wrong Thursday. This was Week 2 Thursday and it meant Games after break. With Mr Hill.

He followed the others into the echoing stink of the changing room, bag slung over his shoulder, and waited outside the office, while his classmates pulled off their sweatshirts and ties. He waited for Mr Hill to finish totting up a row of figures in his register.

'Yes?' he said, hearing Tony's knock. 'What now?'

He said: 'I thought it was Week 1, sir. I haven't got my kit.'

'But you have brought a report card, haven't you, Hudson? Not exactly a brilliant success is it? What is it, the end of the second term and you've forgotten what week we're in?'

'There's been a bit of difficulty at home. Sir.'

'I'm sure there has. There always is. Give us the card then.'

He read the other comments, pulling at the corner of his moustache with his thumb and forefinger. He reached across his desk for a pen.

Carefully he wrote three lines where it said periods 3 and 4.

'Right, lad, you're to go round to Mr Rowan and tell him you're there to collect litter. I shall check with him to see that you've done what you've been asked.'

He'd written: 'Tony didn't bring his kit to the lesson. This meant he couldn't take part in the activities. A complete waste of everyone's time.'

His writing sloped back and was very thin. You had to read it slowly to make sense of the words. He knew that Miss Wilson would make sense of the words. She'd made it clear what he needed to achieve in each lesson or else there would be an after-school detention.

Mr Rowan gave him a grey sack and a metal litter picker. When you squeezed the handle at the top the pincers at the bottom closed together. He was out at the front of the school, pulling bits of paper from the rose bed, when the Head and Mr Carmell came out of the main entrance.

'You've been very helpful,' Mrs Stein was saying, treading lightly down the steps. 'I'll get in touch with Haydon Jones and see about the grant. I'm sure he'll be able to straighten this out.'

'Is that a defaulter I see before me?' said Mr Carmell. He shielded his eyes, was looking at Tony.

'Quite possibly.'

He glanced up at where they were standing.

'You're in Year 9, aren't you?' asked Mrs Stein, her face suddenly serious, forehead creased. Like she'd spotted a large thistle in the garden.

'Yes, miss. Mr Rolph's form.'

'And why are you litter-picking?'

'Forgot my Games kit, miss.'

'Well,' said Mr Carmell, 'you might find it useful to pack your bag the night before school. You know, check through your timetable to make sure you've got all the right stuff.'

Tony looked away at the cars lined up in the car park. Heard the sound of traffic on the main road. He wondered if he was supposed to say anything. He said: 'Yes, sir.'

'Weren't you one of the boys involved in that business over at Ailsworth Heath?' asked Mrs Stein. 'Where everyone had to come home early?'

He looked down. He felt his face go red. 'Yes, miss.'

'And now you've forgotten to bring your kit?'

'Yes, miss.'

'And you're on report, of course?'

'Yes, miss.'

'What's your name?'

'Tony Hudson.'

'Right, Tony Hudson,' said the Head. 'I shall make a point of checking with Miss Wilson how you're progressing with that report card. This is simply not good enough.'

As she turned away, guiding Mr Carmell to his car, he heard the governor say: 'Ailsworth Heath's my neck of the woods now. Or it will be this time next week.'

When he'd first come to the school, along with all his friends in Year 7, it had felt big and strange. On the second day, when he'd got lost in one of the Science corridors, he'd asked for directions at the prep room.

'Lost are you?' said a technician, a large woman in a white coat. Like a doctor in a hospital, he thought. Or a scientist. 'I'll take you there,' she said, when he'd explained he was looking for room 19.

But then, later on that term, during a wet October, he'd called at the front office to hand in a note from Mr Rolph, and Mrs Stevenson, the secretary, had leaned over the counter and said: 'Can you take this visitor to room 32?' – indicating a young woman in a grey coat – 'She needs to talk to Mrs Kaur.' And he'd led her confidently across the school, up the Arts staircase and then down the corridor to the Drama studio.

Now, everything seemed to go into reverse. It was like he was becoming a stranger to the school: no longer a part of a friendly world. Everything was simply coming apart. Like he was lost again.

Even Mr Travis, his Technology teacher, had raised an eyebrow when he'd produced his report card at the start of the lesson. He'd said: 'I heard about all this on Tuesday, Tony. I must admit I was surprised that you'd got yourself involved. You'd better sit down and behave.'

At the end of school he had to wait with Spanier and Clayton outside Miss Wilson's door. They were in different classes.

Spanier pushed his hair out of his eyes. He said: 'How long's that 'un for then?'

'Two weeks.'

'Right. Steven Delaney gave you a soaking I heard.'

He was silent. Looked across the concourse at the glass doors leading into the assembly hall. He said, turning to Spanier, 'Delaney needs to watch himself. He won't be able to run away next time.'

'Oh yeah,' said Spanier, a sneer sliding across his face. 'Says who?' Miss Wilson opened the door. She said: 'Right, Tony Hudson, I want to see you.'

Her office was long and narrow. A window at the far end and her desk pushed against the right-hand wall. She said: 'You can sit there.'

And when he was in his place, she opened a file with his name on it and said: 'Let's see the damage then. So what happened in Games?'

The window glass was slightly frosted so that although it allowed light to enter the room, you couldn't see out. The drone of an electric polisher could be heard in the corridor.

He looked up. Her hair was fair with lines of grey. There were creases radiating from the corners of her eyes.

'I forgot, miss,' he said.

She was silent for a moment, looked back at her record and said: 'That's not good enough, Tony. You were placed on report on Tuesday. It was made very clear to you then that you had to perform properly during lessons and that includes bringing the right equipment to classes.'

There was a photograph of a baby on her windowsill. It had fair hair and was laughing at the camera.

He said: 'Yes, miss.'

'If you can't obey the rules of this school, Tony, then you'll have to stay behind and serve a detention. And I know that you wouldn't want that to happen.'

She turned back to the file.

'I've arranged to write a note to your parents at the end of next week to tell them how you've got on. Let's hope everything will be all right by then and we can simply forget about this unfortunate interlude.' She looked up from her desk. She said: 'Do you understand what I've just said?'

And suddenly he felt very tired, like he'd spent the whole day completing a cross-country run. First Mr Hill, then Mrs Stein and the governor, Spanier and Clayton outside – now this. He rubbed his eyes with his hand. He said: 'Yes, miss.'

He unlocked his bike, slung his leg over the crossbar and pedalled down Furnace Lane. There were ruts and holes in the surface and by the railway bridge someone had aerosoled the faded 'Sound Your Horn' sign.

He waited at the main road for the cars and lorries

to rumble and whine past and then it was over and on to Weston Lane.

He looked at his watch. It was gone four. He wondered whether Michael would be waiting for him. Whether he would still be keen on the idea. Tony wondered what he'd say when Michael asked him the question.

And he thought of Mr Hill and the comment he'd scribbled on his report card; and the way Mr Carmell had looked down at him from the top of the stairs by the entrance. 'Check your timetable and make sure you've got the right stuff,' he'd said, punching the words 'make sure' as if he were pressing buttons on a machine.

He could just see the spire of Hannington church when a dark figure on a bike came into view. A wave of the arm and then: 'Don't tell me old mother Wilson kept you talking!' Michael laughed. 'Come on,' he said, wheeling round. 'Back to the conference room.' He stood up and shouted: 'Wait 'til you see this rat I've found.'

And when they'd examined the corpse and noticed the ridges on its tail, the way its teeth stuck out, they'd climbed up the stack and sat overlooking the old road and the empty fields.

'Look,' said Michael. 'If you slip into school like I told you – sort out the register – we've got a chance of getting across the county and fishing out the mug from the pond. I mean,' – he looked down and tugged at a piece of plastic binding – 'it might be old and it could be worth a bob or two. You know?'

If they got caught or he got found out he could say he was doing it to help his parents. That he wasn't simply skiving school but was trying to do something constructive. And maybe the mug or jug or whatever might actually be valuable. Like it was ancient and made from solid silver.

He listened to the wind blowing against the metal roof, thought of the scowl on Miss Wilson's face, remembered his father.

'OK,' he said at last. 'OK, Michael. You win.' He climbed down. 'I need to get home now, but I'll meet you here tomorrow. Bring stuff to eat and drink.'

'What time?' called Michael, as he cycled off.

'9.20. At the latest.'

Ten

Michael was in front of him, head down and pushing against the wind blowing into their faces. The sky grey and churned with cloud. The road empty. Down, down, down, he said to himself in time with the pedals. On, on, on.

Ahead he could see the great wedge of wood that stretched in a semicircle, light brown with dark spears of pine. Dead elms waymarked the road. Trunks thickened with ivy. Branches like bony stumps.

He listened to the *tick-tick-tick* of his front wheel. The mudguard catching the tyre as it turned. As regular as a clock.

He hadn't taken Michael's advice about going into school. He thought: if I go into school and the Head appears, or I'm stopped by one of the secretaries, or Mr Rolph comes loping down the corridor, I won't know what to say, except that I'm late. And there was all that business about having the right equipment. If he got caught, he'd have to spend the day in class. And he'd need all his Week 2 Friday stuff. And if he didn't get caught there'd be the problem of the extra weight to carry.

Over breakfast his mother had stood with her hands in the sink, looking out over the playing-field, listening to the radio. There was news about a civil war in central Africa. A pigeon was pulling twigs from the silver birch.

She said: 'You've probably worked out that your father is in a bit of bother about the magazine.'

'Money,' he said.

'Yes.' She sighed and looked down, into the water. 'So you'll have to be patient with him.'

'The UN Secretary-General has called for both sides to announce a cease-fire,' said the voice. The pigeon dropped the twig.

'We'll probably pull through OK,' his mum said, but her voice was flat, grey.

'Will we lose the house?'

She turned from the window, her yellow rubber gloves catching the light. 'Where did you get that idea?' she said.

'Dad's got a loud voice.' His cereal had turned to a brown mush. Wet and marshy. 'I overheard him talking to you. Last night.' And then; 'After the phone call.'

'We're a long way from that, Tony,' his mother had said, and placed a dish on the draining board.

'I might be a bit late this evening,' he said.

'Oh?'

'Yes.' He filled his mouth. Tried to sound casual. 'There's an after-school football practice. Thought I might turn up.'

'You'll need your kit then,' she said.

'Yes. Don't worry. I'll get everything sorted out.'

And he'd gone upstairs and taken his boots and Games kit and placed them in the bottom of his wardrobe, beneath the old racing car box.

'Gawd sakes,' said Michael. He was leaning out of his bedroom window. Hair sticking up in tufts. 'I thought you said 9.20 at the barn?'

It was just gone 8.25.

'Change of plan,' he called. 'Come and let me in.'

And then later on, the chat with his mum fading behind like the grey hedge, and Michael alert and pedalling fast, they passed under a high-tension wire and the road began to drop steeply into Calderhay, twisting right and then left, past the wood. They needed to look out for the turn in the village, Tony thought, standing up to catch the crouched figure ahead.

He called, 'Wait at the bridge!' and Michael raised his hand, pressing on.

'What d'you think?'

They sat on the bank, bikes angled against a lamppost. Before them the stream – splashing under the bridge, pulling at a plastic bag hanging from a branch.

'Wind's a problem,' he said.

The houses were stone-built here, and thatched: the straw packed and shaped like hair under a net. He looked at his watch. It was a shade before 9.30. 'We've taken fifty minutes,' he said, unscrewing his water bottle. 'S'pose we could be there, maybe, by about one. Maybe.'

'Then that's OK, isn't it? What time did you tell your old dear you'd get back?'

Michael bent down and threw a stone into the water.

At school they'd have just started English with Mr Rolph. He was going to collect in their homework today. On the character of Romeo. Over on the right, as he stood talking to the class, smiling as he made points with his hand, he'd notice the empty seats, like gaps in a full mouth.

And perhaps he'd say, eyebrow raised, 'Does anyone know where Tony Hudson is today?'

'I said—' and there was the stream, the polished

stones, Michael looking at him. 'Five would be OK.' And then: 'Pushing it any later. Want a drink?' holding out the bottle.

'No problemo, mate,' said Michael, taking a swig and wiping his mouth with his sleeve. 'We'll make it.' Grinning.

More prison camp talk.

'Let's go.'

They pedalled quickly through the village, past the church and the Sawyer's Arms, across the main road and then the steep climb to the wood at Fermyn – pushing through the gears and standing up to keep the cogs turning. And then, breasting the hill, cruising down into the valley, the wind being funnelled into their faces. He could feel rain, the sky darkening.

The police car took them by surprise, just before the quarry and the Oundle junction. They heard the engine and then it was past, and slowing, brake lights flashing and the driver checking his mirror. Then it accelerated away, signalling left.

'Thought he was gonna stop for us there!' said Michael, grinning. 'Don't expect to meet the police on these old roads – eh?'

North of Oundle they picked up the sign for Wansford and for the first time were no longer fighting a headwind, the road undulating slowly downhill into the swampy levels of the Nene.

We're into unknown territory, he thought, we've never come this far. At Oundle the pale stone of the houses, the dusty windows in the shops, seemed light years away from the red brick and hustle of Gretford. Public schoolboys in dark jackets walking in groups; large German cars crowding the market square.

And beyond, the land seemed more open, less packed. Woods no longer filled the horizon, just hedgerows, the flash of rape fields coming into flower, the faded brown of farmhouses.

At Fotheringhay they stopped by the river to look down at the water, big and dark and swollen after the rain. Boiling into eddies. Green shoots of reeds by the side and mallards watching from the bank.

'What's that then, over there?' said Michael, pointing at the mound on the other side. Rising ten metres, a kid's sandcastle in grass.

They checked the map, spreading it out on the bridge.

'Says "motte and bailey". It's the site of an old castle,' Tony said. 'They would have had a keep – you know, some kind of fort on top. Probably to guard this river crossing.' Year 5 History coming back.

'Right. Like the local army?'

'Yeah.'

On, on, on. Listening to the creak of his handlebars whenever he stood up. Feeling the sweat turning cold on his forehead. Waiting for the police siren, following up the report from the squad car they'd seen in the Lyveden valley.

At Nassington, by a wall overhung with chestnut, they propped their bikes and Tony went into Potter's newsagents. There was a sandwich board outside advertising the *Peterborough Echo* and sweet jars crowded the front window.

Inside it was dark, and it took him a minute to adjust to the light. A bell tinkled loudly when he opened the door.

There was the sound of a paper being put down in a back room, uneven footsteps on a stone floor and then a man with white hair and a sharp look limped through the doorway, behind the counter.

'Yes?' He scowled, staring through the thick lenses of his glasses.

Tony picked up two chocolate bars. 'I'll have these. Please.'

The man pressed the keys on the cash register.

'That'll be 64 pence.' And then: 'Why aren't you at school? You should be at school at your age. What are you doing out at this time of day?'

He fumbled with his change and dropped a pound. It rolled away under a rack of wrapping paper. As he bent to pick it up, the bell rang and a large woman in a green coat came into the shop.

'Good morning, Mr Graveny,' she said.

Her voice was brisk and clear. Like someone used to giving orders.

'Ah, I see you've got a customer.'

His fingers closed on the coin.

'Young lad out of school,' the man said, frowning, and they both looked at him. Tony felt the heat on his face as he got to his feet. He handed over the money. He said: 'There's a training day at my school. We don't have to go today.'

'Humph.' The man gave him his change.

The woman said: 'They seem to spend less and less time in school. Always gallivanting about.'

'And up to no good,' the man added. 'You don't come from round here, do you? You and your friend over there.'

'No. We're from Thrapston. Out cycling.' He went to the door. 'Goodbye.'

The old man watched as he gave a chocolate bar to Michael, watched as they got on their bikes and pedalled out of the village.

Later, after Wansford and the road stuck with

frozen traffic, they made the slow climb towards Castor Hanglands and Ailsworth Heath. The first trees appearing over to their right as they changed down, a fringe of brown matching the ploughed fields.

'It's – over – there,' he said, breathless, pointing.

'Thought so,' said Michael.

Other woods, spinnies like islands, to their left.

A transporter went past carrying a yellow bulldozer. The slipstream made their bikes stagger.

'Shouldn't be on a road like this,' he said, pulling his front wheel away from the verge.

He remembered his father, when he was younger. He would sit upright and make a slowing down gesture with his right hand. To speeding cars. Like patting the head of a baby, he'd said. 'Got to make yourself look big,' he'd explained. 'Sit up tall. Like animals when they're in danger.'

At the junction, signed Helpston and Ufford, Michael said: 'I'm taking a leak – won't be a sec,' and he disappeared into a clump of trees.

Tony sat on his saddle and looked back down the road. His knees ached and there was a pain in his calves, like you feel when you get cramp in a swimming pool. He tried not to think of the way south, the road through the towns, the long, slow hills.

He pulled his sleeve back and checked his watch. It had just turned 1.20.

If they found the mug quickly and rested for half an hour, maybe they'd be back by 5.30, he thought. Or six.

He could always phone up. Always say that he'd been invited back to Chris Phillips's house. But then again, his father had spelled out that he was grounded. And grounded didn't mean going back to tea at anyone's house. That was the point of it.

A yellowhammer sat on top of an ash, looking away from him. It pulled its head back and started to sing: 'Little bit of bread and no – cheese.' Michael had pointed that out – something he'd got from his dad.

'Right. Let's go!' said Michael, pulling his bike on to the road.

They met the transporter again at the turning into Castor Hanglands. The driver was leaning out of the cab and talking to a workman wearing a hard hat. He was giving the driver instructions, turning and pointing to the right. He said: 'Follow the track round there. The site office's straight ahead.'

The engine revved and then the load moved on, the great wheels treading the daisies scattered across the border.

The workman picked up a hammer. He was putting up a sign that said something about the

Hanglands Housing Development, but he paid no attention as they pedalled past, heading down towards the trees along the stony, puddled track. They could hear the growl of engines to the right and there was a backhoe digger humping earth beyond the trees.

'Building work maybe,' Tony said.

But at the clearing, by the silver birch trees, where the coach had parked and where Mr Jordan had given out his instructions for their behaviour, there was a wooden sign that they hadn't noticed before. It explained that Ailsworth Heath had been 'designated as a site for rural development'. The land bought for the 'construction of 3,500 units'.

He read it out to Michael. 'They're going to build a housing estate,' he said. 'Probably what those machines are doing. Clearing the land.'

Michael said nothing; he held his bike and looked at the words.

A wood pigeon clattered above them, breaking through the branches.

When Michael turned, his face was unsmiling; he said: 'That name – there,' pointing to the board. 'That's the company that killed my dad.'

There was a black-and-white photograph of a grey-haired man, and the name in bold letters: Carmell

86

Construction. The 'C' of 'Carmell' exaggerated, like a great, curving scythe.

He heard someone shouting in the next field. Like in another world.

Michael brought back his fist and smashed the sign.

Eleven

'It was a Sunday. February 27th. Cold enough to freeze your breath. He was working at the estate. When he phoned he said to Mum he wanted to talk to me. He wasn't really cut out for the phone. Voice too loud, much louder than it needed to be.

'"Michael, is that you?" he said after I'd said "Hello?"

'I could hear someone in the background filling a bucket. Water swooshing against metal, clanging against a sink.

'"Look, old son, I can't get back this afternoon. Richard has had to go home because his wife's sick and with all these ewes about to give birth, someone's got to stay on site."

'"Does that mean I won't see the fish being dropped into the lake?" I said. I was feeling all hot and angry at the same time. And then there's silence at the other end, like in some way I've caught him out. Cut him off at the knees.

'Maybe, just maybe,' – and here Michael's voice became a whisper again, like wind on metal, the bits of words breaking up, fading into the afternoon – 'he was trying to think of something to say, to kind of not make it so painful like. He was never very good at telling me bad news or anything. Like when the rabbit died. I was five, just after I'd started primary school. It was him who climbed the stairs and told me. Sitting on my bed and patting my shoulder. Like that would help.

'Sooooh, he said: "I'll make it up to you, Michael. Never you fear, old son."'

In the silence Tony felt the breeze touch his face, heard a starling rattle in a branch nearby, put together its confused burble. Ahead, the water stretched tight, holding its picture of trees and sky. It was like there were just the two of them left, alone in this wilderness.

Michael cast a stone into the pond. He wiped his eyes with his hand and left an earthy smudge on his face.

'"Never you fear, old son." That's what he said. I never spoke to him again.

'I went kind of blank, like when your hands get really cold when you're chucking snow, that kind of numb. The deep freeze. He was – killed the next day. On the bike – you know the Japanese 500 he had? He'd been up all night with the lambing. Was in bed when I went to school – and he was at work when I got home.'

He leaned forward, head bowed. 'Later, I opened the door to this copper. He took his hat off and everything and he said, "Is your mum in?" and I didn't really make any sense of it then but they went into the lounge and I heard the mumble of the copper and then there was a cry from Mum. Like "Oh no, no, no," like she was trying to shut it all out.

'When he came out he went into the kitchen and filled the kettle up. He turned to me and said, "You're Michael, aren't you?" smiling, like he was a neighbour or something.

'And I said that I was and he said, "Could you be a big help and tell me where the tea's kept and where you have your cups and saucers?"

'And when that was sorted out and everything, he said, "Come and sit down, Michael, I've got something serious I want to say to you."

'And when I sat down, at the table, with my back to the boiler, and he was sitting in the place which Dad used to take, he started talking, and really, when he started – "I've got some really sad news to tell you, Michael," – I kind of knew what he was going to say. That Dad was in an accident. And that he wouldn't be coming home any more. Not tonight, not ever.

'And the whole time the copper was talking, I looked round the kitchen and there were – you know, Dad's red mug on its hook, his scarf on a chair, even his notepad where he used to write out stuff he needed to remember, with the ballpoint. Everything.

'Dad had come out of the estate and just after the bridge at Carnworth there was this lorry that braked to avoid something in the road. It was dark and cold and Dad went into the back of him. Killed straightaway, so they said.

'The police said that the brake lights on the lorry weren't working properly, but all they got for that was a fine. You know, a couple of hundred quid kind of touch.

'Dad must have been travelling too quickly, so they said, at the inquest. Shouldn't have been so close to the lorry. Death by misadventure. The company sent a letter to Mum, after the funeral and that, saying they were sorry about everything. Sorry doesn't change much, does it?' and he lifted his head and looked across at Tony, eyes red, face smeared with dirt.

'No.'

Blackthorn leaves fluttered overhead; a moorhen nosed amongst the reeds. Michael's dad had a red face and wore a flat cap, Tony remembered. Saturday afternoons spent in his greenhouse, bent over seed trays.

Michael's dad showing him how to repair a puncture on his bike. 'Need to take your time,' he'd said.

Michael was talking again.

'That writing – on the sign – that's them. I remember the picture – on their letter – the one they sent to Mum.'

Michael's dad's fingers pulling the inner tube free; feeling inside the tyre for the nail. 'Got to check for the cause,' he'd said, 'else you'll get another 'un.' A shy grin.

'So,' said Michael, looking around. 'They killed Dad and now – and now they're gonna turn over this place,' – and he pointed at the pond in front of them. 'Fill that in and cut down all the trees. Like that estate in Gretford. The Willows.'

'Yes,' Tony said, poking at the mud with a twig. 'Lawnmowers and large cars.'

He looked over at the silver birches, by the gate. Tried to picture what it would be like with the woods gone and the stream elsewhere.

'The worst thing of all,' Michael went on, 'was this package that arrived from Crichton House, afterwards. Some of the things that he'd left behind. It was wrapped up in brown paper, but it was obvious what it was – a Benson pike rod. He said he'd get one for my birthday. I got it early. I never used it. Could hardly bear to touch it, imagine him going to a shop and sorting it out for me. I've not fished since.'

They looked down at the water, at the haze of midges, the pondskater zigzagging amongst blackthorn petals. In the distance the *zing-zing-zing* of a chainsaw meeting bark, trunk, filaments, pulp.

Michael stood up, dusting the seat of his jeans. He looked at Tony. 'We'd better get on with it,' he said.

Twelve

The face on the board had been Mr Carmell, the school governor. He would be the owner of Carmell Construction. The governor who had come into their classroom when Michael had run out into the corridor.

He remembered his uneven teeth, the stink of onion. The finger stabbing at Michael's work. He didn't say anything: Michael wouldn't want any more muddle in his life.

But then Michael said suddenly, 'So, don't let's mess about with bits of stick and all that caper: it's not that deep here,' – and he untied the laces on his trainers, pulled off his socks. 'Time for a paddle, I think,' – a flicker of a smile creasing his face as he rolled up his jeans. 'I should have brought Dad's waders: he'd have liked this.'

And then, 'Garr! It's freeeezing,' as first one foot and then the other slipped beneath the surface, touched leaf-mould, mud, his whole body held tight, fists clenched against the cold.

'Not too far, Michael,' Tony called. 'Just over to your right, metre, metre and a half maybe.'

Circles rippling out from his slow tread, eyes reading the dark.

Plash, plash, the water said.

'It's really soft here,' said Michael. 'Not like sand at the seaside. Ah, what's that?' – stopping his slow, stiff-legged walk, calves buried, left foot probing the pond floor. He bent down, forearms vanishing.

'Piece of rock,' he called, pulling out a streaming, blackened mess, hands covered in dark mud. 'Paw! Absolutely stinks, this stuff!' – chucking the rock aside, bending again and feeling amongst the rot and soft silt, fingers touching twigs, stones, earth.

Above them, a piece of black sky turned slowly about the wood. Head shifting this way, that way. *Craaw-craaw*, it said, *craaw-craaw*, watching the land rotate, primaries like fingers feeling the air.

'I – think – that's – it – there.' Michael pointed to his left, wading forward, more urgently, leaning into the water, above his knees in the water and, '– that's it – here!' – the pile of dark silt glistening in the light, the tapered shape and handle with twigs, leaf-mould, water silvering away.

'Yes!' he shouted. 'Yes!'

Michael turned, waded back, chucking aside mud that splashed in great clumps. Bending at last to wash it free, clean of mess.

And it emerged intact but creased along one side; dark green and in places scarred with holes, like acne, but unmistakably, obviously, a tankard used in an old pub. Tony imagined a low ceiling and greasy candles; men with clay pipes and three-cornered hats. Red faces at the bar and metal tankards. It was like lifting something from an ancient wreck.

'There's some growth – like algae or something,' Tony said, touching the metal.

'Yeah,' said Michael. 'Yeah, we'll need to get it cleaned up. A bit of a polishing and everything. Here – Tone – you hold her – I'll get my feet sorted. It's a cold 'un this.'

Surprisingly light, he thought, feeling the weight in his hands, careful not to hold it by the handle. It was ridged at the top, where the metal was bordered with a kind of lip; two more halfway down, in parallel. The base splayed like a stand. And a great dent in the side, tilting the jug to one side, so that if you placed it on a table it would look like it was staggering, injured.

'Look,' said Michael, trying to wring the water out of the bottom of his jeans, 'let's stuff the jug in the bag and head off back. You know,' – looking up, smiling – 'we got what we came for.'

He took the mug and gave it a last wash in the pool, running his hand round the inside like someone cleaning a glass. Placed it carefully in his rucksack.

They unlocked their bikes from the fence and then pushed past the sign that marked the place of the housing development and pedalled slowly out along the pale yellow earth that led to the road and the beginning of the way south.

As they left the trees and jolted along the track, they saw the smoke of exhaust vents from vehicles working at the far end of the heath; the sound of heavy engines like tractors on an autumn afternoon; two men whacking stakes into the ground.

'This place'll be covered in tarmac before the summer's through,' Tony said.

'Yeah,' said Michael. 'And the creatures'll all be gone. Those leeches we saw? All the birds and stuff? Rubbed out – and no one will give a toss.' He spat into the side of the track. 'Just a load of cack. All of it.'

They cycled in silence, feeling the breeze on their left as they turned south and began the slow descent into the valley of the Nene, the smudge of Southey Wood to their right.

It was 2.10 and he knew there was no chance of getting back before five. Six maybe, but he was conscious of the steady ache in his legs, the way every time he pressed down pain travelled up from his right knee. He leaned back in his saddle, easing his shoulders.

Maybe his father would call the school? Drive over to find out what time the football practice finished? Then what? Call the police? Visit Michael's mum to see what she knew?

They passed a badger flopped dead in the verge, its head smashed. He hadn't noticed that before. Big creature like that, bumbling about in the dark. Then *bang*, is that how it went?

Thirteen

'So, what's this then, boys? Bit of ironmongery you've found to help you with your – ahem – "project"?'

The police officer held the tankard level with his face, turning it round in the light. 'Take your time,' he said, looking at them. 'I can't wait to hear your explanation about this. Family heirloom is it? Something you've dug up as part of an archaeological excavation?' He smiled at them both. 'Look, I was young once, told a few fibs in my time. Let's climb into the vehicle and see if we can agree a story that's a bit closer to reality. And we might as well start with names. OK?'

It was warm in the car and Tony became fully aware of how exhausted he was, not just with the endless pushing of the bike – forearms stretched, standing on the pedals against the wind and the long, tapering hills – but with the fretting about parents and school, the sense of being trapped in someone else's life.

This is the bit in prisoner of war films where the escapees get interrogated, he thought. Where they're supposed to give only name, rank and number. But they'd already given the wrong names and had stumbled straightaway when asked about school.

He looked out of the side window at the straggling line of hawthorn and the faded field beyond, the grass patched yellow and green.

In prisoner of war films, where they escaped over the wire or dug tunnels out of their compounds, there was always a sense of 'home' – that they were escaping from something bad and heading somewhere warm and welcoming and right.

He could see the surprised look in his mother's eyes when she heard the news. That her son had been 'picked up by the police'. Was that how it went? And what of his father, struggling to raise money for the magazine, what would he say? Banging about the dining-room and shouting abuse about being an absolute and utter disgrace?

He closed his eyes and sat back in the seat. Listened to the calm voice of the policeman talking to Michael, his uniform crisp and clean; the car ordered and smelling slightly of oil. Everything in its place. Tidy and structured, as his dad would say.

He thought back to his excitement at starting at

Scratch Brook and his determination to do well, to please his teachers. When he'd turned up in his new sweatshirt and red badge. Working each evening to make sure his homework was neatly written; produced on time.

Now he was sitting in the back of a police car, miles from home on a day when school was speeding towards the end of another week. Not just cack, he thought, looking at Michael in the front seat. Not a word for all this.

'Let's put the notebook away,' said the officer, turning to look at him. 'I want you to tell me your story. Like where you're from and what you've been doing.' His face widened into a smile. 'If it's any help, to get you beyond the uniform and the car and the blue light, I'm a dad as well. I go to football matches of a Saturday and I like a pint down the pub. And I've also been twelve or thirteen.'

A lorry went past and they felt the car shake.

'I wasn't born a policeman you know. My name's Ranjit Singh.' He looked across at Michael. 'And you are?'

Michael looked down, not meeting his gaze. He said; 'We've not committed a crime or anything.'

'Right, well, that's a good start. Where did you find the tankard? It's obviously pretty old.'

'You think so?' said Michael.

'Oh sure. Look at the growth on the side, the design.' He touched it with a forefinger. 'At least a hundred years – maybe a lot more.'

'We found it in a pond, over at Ailsworth Heath,' Tony said.

'Yes? I used to go there myself, when I was a kid. Collecting frogspawn and what not.'

'They're building over it or something,' said Michael. 'We saw this sign and heard the earthmovers – chainsaws.'

'That's right. The new village of Castor Hanglands.' He rubbed his chin and then said: 'Completely wrong, of course.'

They both looked at him.

'Oh yes. You'll never get wetlands and wild heathland like that back again. Thrown aside because it's not earning anyone any money.'

When he was young his parents had told him if he ever became lost, got himself separated from them, he should go to a policeman and ask for help. He said, 'But won't they get me into trouble?' bothered by the dark uniform, the height, the strange, conical helmets.

No, no, they said. They'll look after you. Give you a drink and a biscuit.

He'd never really believed all that of course. At the

102

end of the day they were people in uniform who came to homes and locked people away. Their job was imprisonment, not being friendly to small children. Or truanting schoolboys.

Yet this one was called Ranjit. Who liked a pint and had collected tadpoles. And if Michael could get his feet wet, then so could he, he thought. There's nowhere else to go.

'We saw the mug in the water last Tuesday,' he said to the back of the driver's seat. 'When we came for a school trip to Helpston.'

Michael turned to look at him, staring back over the top of the seat. He didn't speak; his eyes gave no meaning.

'Right,' said the officer, looking down at the mug that he held on the flat of his hand, finger lightly touching the rim.

'There was this – there was trouble. On the trip.'

The policeman looked back. 'OK,' he said.

'Yeah,' said Michael suddenly, 'and we were pushed into the pond. Back on the heath. Got the blame and everything. Got stuffed, the pair of us. He's on report and all. And I'm – well,' – his face red, eyes staring down – 'I'm in front of the governors – next week.'

'Off school?'

'Yeah.' And then: 'We didn't grass up anyone. Neither

103

of us. I mean, it's worse for him because he's never had bother before. Gets on well and everything. I've been round the block a few times.'

'Still hurts though?'

'Just makes me really angry, mister, you know. It's all just "Get out, Michael Slater" and "Where's your report card, Michael Slater?" That's it. Every stinking day.'

The anger was like a sudden storm, Tony thought, all that energy stacked up thousands of metres. The sky gaping and bleeding, spitting light.

He said, quietly: 'We decided to cycle up here from Gretford to see if we could pull the mug out of the pond.'

'Yeah. And we were doing ever so well. Knackered obviously, but what do you expect after all the pedal power and no lunch or anything? And that's it really. That's it, mister.'

Michael leaned back, held out his hands, wrists together, face defiant. 'You can cuff me now.'

Fourteen

He was pushing uphill in the dark. When he looked down his front light was on but it shone with a feeble, emaciated glow, flickering as he went over potholes in the track. The ground disappeared beneath him; there was nothing ahead. And yet the pedalling was getting steadily more difficult. He tried to click down but met only resistance. He was already in the lowest gear and he realised that he'd have to stand up and push if the gradient got worse.

Behind, over his shoulder, he could hear the sound of another bike, close to but out of sight. You could hear the rhythmic clanking of the chain, the noise of the tyres crunching over the uneven surface. Someone was panting behind, like they were having difficulty with the slope, labouring as it got steeper and steeper.

'Keep going,' said a voice. 'Keep – going – they're – catching – up.' And from the echo he realised they were in some kind of tunnel, the voice booming around a roof he couldn't see. The voice that came from his father.

It was saying: 'It's 8.50, Tony.'

A hand shook his shoulder. His father was looking down at him.

'We're going into town to sort out a few things. About the magazine. We should be back by twelve.'

'OK,' he said. 'All right.'

His legs ached and the skin around his face felt tight, as if he'd caught the sun. His rucksack was over by his wardrobe. The squadron was still headed south.

The copper had actually smiled when Michael held out his hands. He'd said: 'I think we're getting a bit ahead of ourselves. Handcuffs and prison later, first we need to review the circumstances.'

'What's that mean?' said Michael, his chin stuck out aggressively.

'Well,' he said slowly, 'there are different ways of looking at the situation, at most situations really. On the one hand we can see a police officer stopping two young cyclists on a weekday afternoon. They immediately lie to him about their names and what they're doing—'

'But—'

'Further questioning reveals that one of them has

106

recently been in serious trouble at his school and has been told to stay away until he's been interviewed by school governors. The other individual has also been in trouble at school, has been placed on report and has been grounded by his parents. He's decided to truant and go cycling. In their possession the officer discovers an old tankard which the youths claim they "found".'

'We did, mister—'

He raised his hand, palm outwards. He said: 'As I was pointing out, there are different ways of looking at any situation. An alternative view might see two quite young boys who had made a potentially important historical find and had worked out a way of recovering it. In doing so, they exercised great ingenuity and physical courage. One of the boys took the risk of getting into further trouble with his parents and with the school. A set of problems that will soon need to be confronted and dealt with.'

He stopped talking and silence filled the car like warm sunshine after a storm. A large bee banged against the windscreen, bounced off like a bullet.

'So, you're not going to arrest us – or anything?' said Tony.

'What for? As your friend said, you've committed no crime.'

'So – you think the mug there's valuable – worth a few bob – that kind of thing?' Michael's eyes were wide with expectation. As he spoke, so his fingers touched the tankard still sitting on the policeman's palm.

'Boys, you've not looked at it very carefully. Here, hold it up to the light and through the grime, the green covering – well, what do you notice?'

He leaned forward between the two seats, both of them looking to where the copper's finger touched the side of the tankard, underlining the dirt. And very faintly, he read: '1820.' He said, 'The writing says "1820"!'

'So it's—'

'At least 180 years old, Michael. Almost two centuries. Now, I'm not an expert, but I would have thought that something like this might have a story to tell. You might want to know why a tankard that was probably quite common – at least in design – was engraved with a date. Another thing that would be worth discovering is whether there's more writing on the metal. Might there be a name, for instance?'

'We could clean it up? See what it's got to say?'

He smiled across the seat. 'You have responsibility for this item now. It's up to you to do the detective work, but I wouldn't try to do the cleaning yourselves.

Try the museum. In Gretford.'

And Tony thought of the old Victorian building at the back of the library. The last time he'd been in there, in junior school, it had been full of rusting agricultural implements – ploughshares and rakes and hedging devices.

'Go in there with your find. Ask if you can see a curator or some expert who might help you.'

He heard the front door slam and seconds later the clang of the gate. His parents were walking into town. If he got up and went into the spare bedroom he'd see them striding smartly down the road, his father's head turned down in conversation with his mother. He'd be telling her about work, about the finances, about what they might do, about what they couldn't. He had been wearing his blue suit, so maybe, even though it was a Saturday, they had arranged to see the bank manager.

He lay back and for the ten thousandth time looked up at his planes on their eternal journey. Once, even two weeks ago, they'd been this reassuring fleet travelling across his room to some unknown destination. Planes of all ages and types, gradually building up layers of dust and fluff that rested on their upper surfaces. There was a P.51 Mustang, a Douglas

Dakota and three different types of Spitfire. Jockeying for position, contrails streaming from their wing tips. They'd travelled from his past, from the very first model he'd put together, into the level flight of the present.

Would they still be flying from this room in a few weeks' time? If the magazine was losing money, like his father had said, did that mean they'd have to move to another house? Would they live in a council house, like Michael, over on the Scratch Brook estate?

How would that feel? Steven Delaney lived there as well, with goons like Spanier and Clayton. The lads who gathered on the corner by the railway bridge and flicked dog-ends at the Year 7 kids. The lads who'd been chucked out last summer for booting an old hedgehog around the playing-field as though it were a football.

'We thought it were dead, Mr Colquhoun,' Spanier had said, lank hair hanging in front of his eyes.

But then there was Michael and he wasn't like that.

Officer Singh had passed the tankard across the front seat. He said: 'You have a big responsibility for looking after this gift from the past. Don't let yourselves down. All of us must take responsibility for everything we do. Look, I will contact my control to see whether I have time to take you and your bikes back to Gretford, to save you the long ride home.'

He flicked a switch on the radio positioned in the well below the dashboard. He said: 'C J Zero 3.'

A voice said: 'Go ahead, Zero 3.'

'I'm just south of Elton, past the railway bridge. Can you run a misspers check for me?'

'Go ahead.'

'A Michael Slater and a Tony Hudson. Both Gretford.'

He'd scuffed the skin on the back of his hand. Patches of blood had dried on his knuckles. From where he'd parked his bike against the fence. Hours ago.

The voice said: 'Nothing reported, Zero 3.'

'Thanks. I'm going off the patch now. To drop two lads in Gretford.'

'OK, Zero 3.'

And they'd gone on to Carnworth: the woodland and fields, the slow hills and the smell of rain in the air, all turned into widescreen TV.

'This'll do you?' the copper said, pulling into the layby just past the Red Lion, and he'd lifted their bikes on to the cycle path, quietly smiling as he turned the estate in a wide sweep before the stilled traffic, right hand raised in farewell.

'Bit of a let-off,' Tony said.

'Yeah,' said Michael. 'But look what we've got! Look what we've brought back! – Let's go amigo!' – and he pushed off into the afternoon, head down and leaning into the bend by the old river bridge.

Fifteen

He sat at the keyboard in the dining-room. Clicked on to a new file. Typed:

> *22 Scotton Road*
> *Grefford*
> *Northants*

Moved the cursor up and changed the first 'f' in Grefford to a 't'.

What else? The date needed to go at the top; somewhere near the address. Or might it go on the other side?

Return.

Sunday 28th March

Yet it looked odd, isolated over on the left, cut off from the rest of the letter. He pushed it over with the space bar so that it became a line underneath the address. Like moving trucks on a railway, he thought. Shunting words.

113

He looked down at the note he'd written on a page torn from his school jotter. It said:

Dear Mr Rolph
Tony was absent on Friday because he had a stomache upset.

Yours Sincerely

He started tapping in the words, listening all the time for the sound of a car pulling off the road, the *crunch-crunch* of rubber on gravel, the sudden silence, two slams.

The dining-room door was stretched back.

In the car the copper had talked about responsibility and everything. Stuff that they'd have to confront and deal with. But how could you deal with truanting on top of a report card? The next step would be an appointment with Mrs Tudor, the woman from the education service, who spent time with 'problem students'. Like Michael.

Outside, wandering over the vegetable patch, there were half a dozen starlings, pecking the ground, moving amongst the green leaves of the cabbages his father had planted that last weekend.

'Got to be a life outside the office,' he'd said, reaching into the wooden seed tray.

Yet there was a letter by his father's coffee cup, to the left of the computer. It was from the bank. It said: 'Re: overdraft facility'. Which meant it was about some of the money that was owed.

And now there were the starlings, like a group of accountants, playing fast and loose with the regulations, wandering over the freshly dug earth, looking for wriggling signs of life.

He clicked the spell checker. Corrected 'stomache'. Sat back and looked at the message. It felt too brief, he thought. But what else could you add beyond the single line? He moved the cursor up to where it said 'upset'. He looked down at the keys, hoping that a particular pattern of letters might turn themselves into phrases, sentences, like starlings settling on to a lawn.

He deleted the full stop and added:

but he should be alright now.

What he wanted to write, of course, was the fact that he had been forced to take the day off school, had made a humungous journey with Michael Slater and had returned with a battered old tankard that was probably going to be of enormous historical importance.

'You've got to be kidding me,' Mr Rolph would have said, looming above him like a bald-headed eagle, his great hooked nose jutting out like a piece of carved rock. 'Go and see Miss Wilson. Immediately.'

No happy landing there, he thought. No phone calls to the museum to get the chief curator over pronto. Just the walk down the corridor to get your life sorted and filed by the cool and thoughtful Year Head. She of the greying hair and crows' feet eyes.

Should it be 'faithfully', he wondered. Wasn't 'sincerely' a word you used when you were writing to people you knew? And his mother didn't really 'know' Mr Rolph, not like friends, at any rate.

He deleted 'Sincerely', typed in 'Faithfully'.

That made it sound more important, more official: the real thing.

Yesterday, still feeling stiff and tired from the bike ride, he and Michael had gone into town early, the tankard wrapped in newspaper and hanging from a plastic carrier bag that swung back and forth, like a pendulum, from Michael's handlebars.

'Be back for lunch,' Michael's mother had called as they'd pedalled away. 'I'm going out at one.'

They strapped their bikes to the railings outside the Sikh temple at the end of the High Street and stopped, as ever, to look in at X-Ray Games; staring down at the front window that was piled with three shelves of consoles. A monitor broadcasting a car chase in 64-bit.

'Great graphics,' he'd said, watching the flashing city streets and scurrying pedestrians.

'Yeah,' said Michael, crossing by the entrance to look in at the other window. 'And a great price.'

When he stood away, he could see their full-length reflections staring back, like shadowy negatives. Michael still wore yesterday's jeans. There was a splodge of pond muck stuck to the bottom of one trouser leg; it was darker than ordinary dirt, more like an oil stain from his bike. And amongst the crowd behind them, perhaps his mother and father. Who might have finished with the bank. Might now be slowly walking towards them.

'Come on,' he said. 'Let's go to the museum – get it over with.'

He wasn't really sure of the procedure. Who they might talk to. What they needed to say. And there was the fear that they'd simply wasted their time. That the tankard was as interesting as an old tyre dropped into a convenient pond.

They walked down the High Street. Past the market stalls and through the pushing crowds trying to buy cheap vegetables, meat, second-hand books.

The museum was in the old part of the town, beyond the market square and squeezed between the library and the parish church. They went up the cobbled slope, under the branches of the dark churchyard trees and in through the framed door.

The woman behind the counter wore a blue jacket and had a red, white and blue scarf. It glistened in the light, like a waterfall tumbling down her neck. Her hair was pale brown and the overhead neon made it shine brightly. When she looked up and saw them, her smile was like a burst of sunshine. Like one of those models you see on adverts, he thought. The ones that say, 'How can I help you?' and 'Have a nice day,' as they showed you the door.

Michael cleared his throat. He said: 'We'd like to see someone – someone who can help us. With this thing. That we've found.'

'Yes?' she said, continuing to smile, 'and what's that?'

Michael reached into the carrier and lifted the newspaper parcel, placing it carefully on the desk. His hands were shaking, Tony noticed, as he pulled the paper away, like he was nervous about talking to this woman, explaining the situation.

The reception desk became covered with sheets of the *Gretford Mercury*, until at last, standing lopsidedly on the grey columns, stood the old tankard – dirty, dented, green. And slightly drunk.

'That looks really interesting,' said the woman. 'And very old.' She smiled again. 'Where did you find it?'

'Yesterday—' Michael began.

'On a field trip. To Ailsworth Heath,' Tony said.

'Yeah,' said Michael. 'In a pond.'

'There's a date carved on one side,' Tony said, moving next to Michael.

'Yeah.' Michael lifted the tankard, held it to the light. 'It's here somewheres – there,' – looking down at her, pointing. 'See? It says "1820" – and well—'

'We thought that there might be more writing on it. We wanted someone to have a look at it for us. Help us. Get it clean.'

The woman touched the green metal and a piece of dirt rattled on to the paper.

'It does look old,' she said. 'But,' – looking up at them, her mouth stretched in apology – 'I'm not an expert. You'll have to talk to someone in Northampton. One of the curators. They could tell you about it.' She smiled. 'You can imagine an old pirate swigging beer from one of these,' she said.

And again the image of the low-ceilinged pub, the yellow light and the crowded bar came back. People talking in thick accents. The sound of laughter.

'How do we – you know—' Michael began.

'See a curator?' she said, and reached for a plastic file on her left. 'The number is – I'll write it down for you – Northampton 7132148. The County Curator is Janet Wilberforce – but if you call them – they're based in Guildhall Road – someone should be able to help.'

'They – em – wouldn't be there. Today?' said Michael, his eyebrows pulled together in disappointment.

'I'm afraid not,' she said. 'Monday to Friday. Nine to five.'

'Right, thank you,' Tony said and took the scrap of yellow paper she held out. He didn't know what else to say, how to end the conversation. Michael wrapped the tankard in silence.

He clicked up the print dialogue box, and pressed 'OK'. The starlings were still scattered across the garden, wandering amongst the beans and spilling on to the lawn. Hands behind their backs, beaks stabbing the grass.

Ten seconds later he was looking down at his absence letter. The words seemed OK but the writing was all huddled in the top third of the page as if the words had taken fright at the great expanse of white.

He went back to the monitor, checked print preview. Pressed 'return' five times, dropping the text so that it was now placed centrally on the sheet. Clear, upfront, in your face. Untrue.

He clicked 'OK' to action the print.

Outside a car stopped and he held his breath, straining to listen above the sound of the paper passing through the rollers. Some voices. A door slammed; his finger hovered over the escape key, eyes watching the letter feeding on to the tray.

The car drove off and again there was silence.

They hadn't spoken as they'd walked back up the High Street from the museum. He could only think of the hours they'd spent pushing at their pedals; the hours of worry about getting back; the thought of school on Monday. The questions from Mr Rolph and Miss Wilson.

'Bit of a waste of time,' he said as they turned towards the precinct.

'Yeah,' said Michael.

'And then I've got to sort out school. For Monday.'

'Should've done what I told you,' said Michael.

That could have made it worse, Tony thought. Maybe got caught out. Shown the door – like Michael. A meeting with the governors. How could you ever come back from that? The jeers of Delaney and Kevin Douglas; doubt and suspicion from teachers. He'd seen it all before, watching Michael stagger through his school career.

They went through the glass doors.

'You know,' said Michael, nudging his arm, '– it's not the end of the world. Got to be a bit – patient – like – like when you're out on a bank, line baited and the rain tipping down. Wet and cold in August. Just have to keep feeding the water – enjoy the scenery. Nothing else for it. No good putting your fist into a wall.' He grinned back at Tony. 'No point in beating yourself up.'

They headed like migrating fish for Taylors, the model shop, and had just drawn level with the fountain when a voice burst through the mutter and chat of the crowded concourse.

It said: 'Been shopping for Mummy and Daddy?'

Delaney lounged in one of the corner seats, arms stretched to either side, along the ledge. Spanier, next to him, grinning back.

'Oh, silly me,' said Delaney, his teeth flashing a smile, 'I forgot. You haven't got a daddy.'

Tony moved to hold Michael's arm, but his friend stopped and simply said, 'Yeah. That's right, Delaney. You're spot on. I've been shopping for my dad.' People passed in front of them. 'Do you have a problem with that?' – eyebrow raised, grin like a crack in a wall.

Spanier shook the hair out of his eyes. He nudged Delaney: 'What's he on?'

'It's in the bag,' said Michael, pointing. 'Like you said.'

'He's touched,' said Spanier, tapping the side of his head.

'Has difficulty standing on his feet,' said Delaney, stretching his arms. 'So I've heard.'

'Anytime, Delaney,' said Michael. 'You know where I live.'

And they walked off, past the hi-fi shop, the chemists and the new outlet selling cut-price phones. All the way to the lift and the second floor.

Which is where they met his parents.

Sixteen

'R' he wrote, using the ballpoint he'd found in the kitchen. And then again, 'R'.

He looked at the signature in his homework diary. His letter was about the right size but in the original the pen seemed to have travelled up through the first downstroke and then curved out boldly before knotting itself and stepping forward like someone's right leg.

His version made the first stroke separate from the rounded bit. It didn't look anything like the 'R' of 'Rebecca'.

Of course what he should have done, if he'd half a brain, was to have made a few copies of the letter so that if he made a mistake with the signature he'd have other versions as spares. He should have saved it as well. He looked at the printout to his right, carefully spaced and clean.

His mother's writing was clear and curved and

touched the paper lightly. There was no sense of uncertainty about any of the letters; no wobbles or awkward joins. The hand was larger than his own, which looked small and cramped and untidy.

In his homework diary, his letters didn't seem to be all the same size and they didn't attach themselves very well to their partners.

'R' he wrote again. And again, his tongue pressed between his teeth, glancing up in between each attempt to check the original. Like trying to get inside someone else's skin, he thought, leaning back to compare the line.

He tried 'Rebecca' and immediately felt uneasy, like he'd committed a crime; like this was some kind of theft. Stealing someone else's identity. And then he thought of school in the morning and Mr Rolph's welcome – 'Ah, Tony. Good to see you back. Do you have an absence note?' – and tried 'Rebecca' again, trying to vary the weight he placed on each of the 'c's.

'This is hopeless,' he said out loud, pushing the sheet aside.

There was no alternative: he would have to start again. Switch on the computer; wait for it to go through its endless checking routine; set up a new file and clean page and then type out another version of the letter. And print off at least half a dozen copies. Before destroying the electronic file and shutting down the pathetic machine.

It was 11.38.

When they'd met his parents in the precinct, his mother had said: 'Oh, Tony – what are you two doing down town?'

His father a tall, silent shadow in his dark suit.

'Doing some research,' said Michael. And then, as if to cover another possibility, 'Good thing I met him – I needed help.'

His father's forehead creased into a frown. Like ripples covering a beach.

'You're Michael?' he said.

'Yeah. That's right, Mr Hudson. You've met me before – I'm easy to forget.' He smiled up at his father.

'Of course you're not,' said his mother, attaching a bright smile to her face. 'Look, Tony, it's lucky that we've met like this because we're going to be late back, I think. We've still got some business to do – we may need to go over to Market Harborough. Can you take care of lunch?'

'Just one second, Rebecca,' his father said. 'I'm wondering whether it wouldn't be a bad idea to take Tony with us?'

They looked at his father, standing with his back to the lift, the numbers flashing above his head every two or three seconds, '4' and then '3' and then '2'. Like it was some kind of countdown.

Michael swung his bag and said: 'Look – got to go now. Thanks for your help.' And then, to his parents; 'Nice to see you again,' and turned away.

'Bye, Michael,' his mother said to the retreating back, the blue sweatshirt immediately lost to sight in the crowd, like a stone dropped over the bridge at Fotheringhay.

'Could we just step aside for a moment?' His father, frowning openly now, moved away from the gaping lift door, and walked to the corner by the old café.

'I don't know what you think you're playing at, Tony, but I explicitly told you, four days ago, that you were grounded for a month and that you were to have nothing to do with the Slater boy. So what's going on?'

He looked down. Hoped that no one from school was passing. 'Don't know,' he mumbled.

'We go out for a couple of hours and then walk straight into you disobeying a set of instructions. What is happening? What do you think you're playing at?'

His father looked at him the whole time he was speaking and Tony knew that if they were at home he'd have been shouting. There was a strained emphasis about the words, a sense of tension – like you feel whenever there's a storm approaching but it's not quite time to unpack the hail and lightning.

'Let's deal with this later,' said his mum, looking at her watch and touching his father on the arm. 'Let's go and get a coffee and talk through the bank details.'

His father turned his head to look at her and then back.

'We've got enough on our plate, Tony,' he said. 'Without having to worry about you getting into further trouble at school.' And then, the tone lightening slightly: 'Did you come by bike? Yes? Right, collect your bike and go home and stay there until we get back.' He paused, rubbing his eyes. 'Do I make myself clear?'

'Yes,' he said. 'Yes. I understand.' Like any other style of conversation had been squeezed out. Like his role was to answer clearly and not use too many words.

Which was of course where Michael was so different. Whenever he got into trouble, every time he got told off by the teachers, he would always try and argue his point of view, get his voice heard. Simply breaking the rules of what was sensible, making a bad situation worse.

As he walked back to the temple and his bike, he thought that survival depended on knowing when to speak and what to say. And how to say it. Think before you speak – maybe that was the secret.

He switched on the computer from the wall socket, pressed the button on the printer and waited for the password signal to appear. Listened to the sound of the fan and watched next door's cat slinking through the gap in the fence. It stopped and crouched down, studying a female blackbird that was standing, head cocked, on the lawn.

His parents had said little about the meeting with the bank manager on Saturday, but when they had gone out two hours ago, it was to talk to estate agents.

He'd wanted to say, 'What happened at the bank?' but he wasn't sure how much he was supposed to know. And whether they were all talking to each other again.

And if they were to sell the house, where might they be living? And what would his father be doing for a job if the magazine was no good?

The page came up and he started tapping in the words, pausing to look down each time he needed to change a letter. The page filling up like a beach covered with dark scraps of weed. Touching the keys in sudden, deliberate stabs. Like the birds on the lawn.

Michael had taken the tankard with him when he'd left the precinct. Tony had watched the carrier swinging backwards and forwards as he listened to his father. Seeing Michael weave between the pushchairs and couples; kick an orange juice carton – and then push on towards the glass doors and the exit by the bus stop.

Yet ten minutes after Tony had cycled home, sitting at the kitchen table, flicking through the pages of *Break Away*, the back-door bell had sounded.

'Hi!' said Michael. 'Thought I'd drop by and see how you'd got on, with your parents and that. Could tell it was heavy which is why I scarpered. They said they might push off for a couple of hours – so what's going on?'

He was still holding the grey carrier, his bike propped against the garage wall behind.

Tony said: 'Look, Michael, do something about the bike – I mean—'

'Bit obvious?'

'Yeah – they might come back.'

He felt embarrassed at having to talk like this, like they were having to watch everything they did. Like taking part in one of those stupid war films where people were on the lookout all the time. In case the enemy discovered the tunnel that was being dug.

Michael passed over the bag and then cycled back down Scotton Road and attached his bike to the first lamppost past the corner shop.

'Should be OK there,' Michael said, slightly breathless from running back, and then, when they were sat round the kitchen table, asked: 'What do you think?'

'About what?' Tony said.

It was like Michael was working to a different plot to everyone else and that he expected you to know at which stage of the story he'd arrived at. Like when they met before school and he assumed the logical thing was to get back to Ailsworth Heath.

'You know,' he said, smiling, and pointing to the carrier. 'You know – about that Mrs Wilberforce and the curators. In Northampton. What do you think?'

'Oh, that.' He touched the carrier. 'Dunno. Give them a call next week. Like the woman at the—'

'Naw. Not that. Take too long, mate. We've got to act now. So. Where's the phone book?'

He wanted to look up Mrs Wilberforce in the directory. Talk to her at home.

'You want to talk to her. At home?' Tony said.

'Yeah. Oh, don't get up – I see it,' and he went over

131

to the dresser and picked up the book, flicking through it with his thumb.

There were two slips of paper marking places that his father had probably inserted. They were in the business section at the front.

It was like Michael had suddenly taken over the house. Arriving and deciding on what to do. Wanting to use the phone without giving a second thought to Tony's parents returning – who might come in through the back door and catch them out.

'W,' said Michael. 'Let me see.'

'Here, give it over. I'll have a look.'

'Yeah,' he said. 'Otherwise we'd be here until teatime and then none the wiser. I need a drink. Mind if I take a swallow of your orange?'

Wight, Wigmore, Wignell, Wilberforce. Wilberforce B; Wilberforce R; Wilberforce T. No Wilberforce J.

'Any luck?' said Michael, wiping his mouth.

'Just three entries. No Wilberforce J.' He looked down. 'One lives in Gretford, one over in Rushden. One in Northampton.'

'Right. Right,' said Michael. 'Could be any. Could be the married whatsit. You know, change of name and all that.'

He was like a tracker-dog, Tony thought. Sniffing at clues, not thrown by dead ends. Tail up, head down.

Michael leaned over his shoulder and followed the entries that Tony indicated.

And then, draining his glass, said: 'Let's phone them all, mate. Nothing to lose, eh?'

He thought of his father checking through the phone bill, ticking off the entries, seeing which numbers were being used. But there were zillions of numbers he got from the phone company and surely – surely? – he wouldn't be able to check each one?

'Where's the phone, mate?'

'There's an extension on the wall,' he said, pointing to the receiver by the door.

And then: 'I'll write the numbers out for you so that you'll be able to read them easily enough.'

'Nar – read 'em out, mate. Nice and clear. That'll do just fine.'

He read the first number carefully, watching as Michael looked at the pad and tapped the keys, pausing between each like a typist uncertain of the letters on a keyboard.

'It's ringing,' he said. And then: 'Hello, could I speak to – er – Mrs Wilberforce?' There was silence for ten seconds. Then, 'Right. All right. Thank you,' and he replaced the receiver.

'No Mrs Wilberforce at that address. A Brian Wilberforce used to live there but he's moved. OK then, give us the next.' Smiling across the kitchen when he could hear the ringing tone at the other end.

'Hello? Oh hi, look, I wanted to talk to Mrs Wilberforce? Yeah, that's right. A Mrs J Wilberforce. Who –? Oh, oh, hello. Well, look, I'm sorry to call you at the weekend and everything, but – yes, yes, well – I'm at school and it's – if you could let – I'd like to explain. I think – look I think you'd be interested. Yes. Yes. I'll be really short and that. I've discovered – well, my friend – yeah, we're fourteen. I'm fifteen next October. – We found this old tankard. Up on Ailsworth Heath, near to Helpston. And it's got a date on it and everything and we thought that – 1820. Yes. Yes I'm sure. There's more writing I think and – it's pretty – we didn't want to damage it or anything – but – yes, yes – I get home from school at about four o'clock most days. Tuesday. Yes. Yes. I could do that. 104, Brighton Road, Gretford. Yeah. It's on the Scratch Brook estate. OK. OK. Thanks and – bye.'

He lifted the receiver from his ear and carefully placed it on the cradle on the wall.

'Funny old bat,' he said quietly, coming to sit down at the table. 'Most particular about the date; kept on repeating, "You did say Ailsworth Heath, didn't you?" as if I shouldn't know where we found it.'

'And?'

'She's calling in to my house. Tuesday at about 4.30. Fancy slipping the guard and coming round?'

Seventeen

Instantly he was awake. Orange light from the street cutting between his curtains. 12.40 on the clock radio. The colon separating the hour and minutes flashing like a pulse. The planes overhead dark shadows, high against the cloud base.

He pushed back his duvet, swung his legs over the side of the bed. Could he risk switching on the light? The clock flicked to 12.41. You could hear cars swishing past on Westfield Avenue. Like a distant sea.

He felt for the light switch, closed his eyes and pressed hard. No sound from down the corridor. The room cast brown with deep shadows. He went over to his school bag, placing each foot carefully, one in front of the other, feeling the weight spread evenly.

He brought it back to the bed, looking inside for the jotter.

The rough copy of signatures wasn't there.

He reached into the bag, less conscious of the

noise now, and pulled out his exercise books, flicking through each in turn, seeing a frantic blur of maths numbers, science diagrams and patiently coloured maps. Everything he'd need for Monday. Except for the rough copy of signatures.

He'd left it downstairs in the dining-room. Somewhere on the table or the floor. Or in the wastepaper basket.

His father was gone by 7.00 most days. His mother in the kitchen fixing breakfast at half-six. Grey light and the steaming kettle. And he asleep.

He needed to get to the dining-room and find the paper before his father rushed in, bad-tempered from lack of sleep and distracted about work, looked down and saw the string of counterfeit Rebecca Hudsons.

His slippers were by his bed, his dressing gown on the back of the door. Like a huge bat at roost.

He needed to go down the stairs and sift through the stuff in the dining-room whilst everyone was asleep.

He'd finished the absence letter an hour before his parents had arrived back. Completing the signature at the sixth shaky attempt and folding the sheet into three to fit one of the envelopes he'd found stacked in the box beneath the table.

He was up in his room, flicking through an old copy

137

of *Big Byte*, when he heard the rattle of the diesel knocking away outside, the single slam and the car fading away down Scotton. Footsteps on the stairs and then his mother tapping on his door.

'I need to speak to you, Tony,' she said, coming in and sitting on his bed.

His first thought, as he looked up in alarm, was that she'd suddenly found out about Friday, had maybe bumped into Mrs Slater and heard from her that they'd dropped school and gone off for the day.

Instead she said: 'We went to talk to the bank manager yesterday morning.'

And he realised that she was going to explain the problem about the money to him. What they were going to do.

'Yes. It's not something I need you to worry about, or anything. But you do need to know what we're planning. So that it's not a great surprise. Or anything like that.'

Her voice was quiet, and the rims of her eyes red. Like she'd been crying.

She was silent for a moment and he placed the magazine carefully on his desk, like that was the polite thing to do when someone was speaking to you on an important matter.

'The problem we've got at the moment, Tony, is about cash flow.'

'Oh yes?'

'It's simply that we're owed a lot of money and we're having difficulty in getting hold of it – from lots of small advertisers. In fact we were out yesterday trying to get people to pay what's overdue – but with little success, I'm afraid.'

When she'd said 'cash flow' he'd had this image of a great surging brown tide, like a river in South America, or somewhere like that, but that instead of water, it was made up of a moving stream of bank notes, rolling and tumbling over each other. And they were in a boat, but they couldn't control it properly and it seemed to be sinking, so that as fast as anyone could chuck money out, more and more seemed to wash in over the side and the boat got lower and lower so that you could imagine everything just sinking beneath the waves and vanishing. Just the dry rustle of a billion bank notes rising and falling; the dead faces of the old Queen shuffling this way and that.

He reached across and picked up a pencil, started to draw stickmen on the magazine cover. His mother was still talking, and when he looked across, her face was turned down, as though she was reading from a script. As though she found this part difficult to put into words.

She said: 'The bank will help us pay the finance

company but they want us to sell the house so that we can pay them what we owe . . .'

On the cover of the magazine there was a picture of a huge gorilla hanging on to the Empire State Building with one hand and clutching a computer monitor with the other. The caption said: 'Can YOU tackle Kong?'

'. . . it's very – very difficult,' she was saying. 'We're all a bit tense – especially Dad. I think he feels that our lives are owned by other people. Which, in a strange way, is true, I suppose. But – well – the estate agent will be visiting the house tomorrow morning to provide us with a valuation – before it's put up for sale.'

Things were happening so quickly. One moment he was lying on his bed watching his aircraft and wondering about the tankard and now the house was going to be sold and—

'Where will we live?'

His mother gave him a sharp look. She said: 'You haven't been listening to what I've been saying, have you?'

'No, no it's not that. I was—'

Her face softened.

She came over and ruffled his hair. 'Somewhere in Gretford, I expect. So as not to mess up your schooling.' And then, hunching down so that her face was on a level with his: 'Don't worry, Tony. This is what life is all about. We'll get everything sorted.'

He looked into her face and then away, out of the window, down the hill towards Westfield Avenue and the factory buildings. He knew that she was trying to comfort him, trying to tell him that this story was going to have a happy ending. That they wouldn't finish up with nowhere to live or no job to provide the cash with which to buy another place.

He said quickly: 'Where's Dad?'

'He's quite – agitated – at the moment. There's a lot to be done – what with the house and the finance company. And he's still got to get the proofs of the magazine to Northampton for this Thursday. So—'

'He's gone out for a think?'

'Yes,' she said. 'Something like that.'

Hours later she was asleep, three metres away. His foot touching the first step, right hand feeling for the banister. He waited, listening to the breathing coming from his parents' room. Their door two-thirds open; their dark drenched in the green light thrown by the radio.

Left foot down, slowly easing his weight on to his left leg; feeling for a loose board; the creak of someone moving on the staircase. And then again. And again.

Stopping on the third as the wood gave a long, stretched-out cry. Ears straining in the dark, waiting for the breathing to stop. Listening for feet on the floor, for the light to flash, for—

But nothing. Silence until the point where the stairs turned back on themselves; where the large copper vase squatted in the corner and where his foot crashed like a hammer to bang out a great hollow *boooooom*.

The dark moved swiftly all around. Big, black, soft, velvety night. He stood motionless. Waiting. Listening. Feeling the soft tread of the carpet beneath his feet.

Someone coughed. Turned over. And then. And then the breathing resumed.

There was no other sound.

It was six steps down to the corridor opposite the dining-room. Faint light from the windows bouncing off the floor tiles. One and two and three and four. He counted down, moving quickly now, feeling more confident, more reckless. Six. The cool of the tiles and then the carpet of the dining-room.

He felt for the edge of the large table, his fingers touching wood as he moved round to where the monitor sat, the pulled back office chair. Looked out into the night. Saw the faint glow of stars speckling the sky.

Where he had been working his hands plunged into

darkness, seeking out the page torn from his jotter. But the table was clear. A couple of pens rolled away. The keyboard rattled its plastic.

The waste bin was to the left, by the windowsill.

He reached out and touched cool stone and at that moment his foot felt the smooth surface of paper. He heard its faint rustle. And as he stretched down to grasp it, so there was a sharp click, the windows turned black and his father stood in the doorway, hair ruffled and anger scarring his face.

Eighteen

His father said: 'What do you think you're playing at? Wandering round the house at one o'clock in the morning? What's going on?'

He felt the paper beneath his feet. Thought about the line of false signatures. He reached for the truth.

He said: 'I couldn't sleep. I was worried. About—'

His father put his hand up, palm outwards. He came into the room, pulled back one of the dining chairs and sat down.

He said: 'I know it's a very worrying time, Tony,' – he made a sweeping gesture with his left arm. 'I don't want you to – you to – well, get yourself in a state – over all this.' A weak smile trickled across his face, like oil on water.

'I know in the middle of the night everything looks bleak. But we'll live to fight another day. Honestly.' A faint flicker of a winter sun. 'Your mum and myself have done the talking. We've made the decisions. We're going in the right direction.' Pause. 'We're not lost, you know that? OK, son?'

'OK,' he said, his foot firmly planted on a string of lies.

'Well,' his father went on. 'Why don't I go and bang some milk in the microwave. Make some malted. Does that sound OK?'

Tony looked across the table at the serious gaze, the faint pleading expression. He knew that this meant his father was trying to make friends, to get everything sorted out.

He said: 'Really good, Dad.'

And when his father had got up and left the room, he was able to look down at the page torn from his exercise book and then screw it into a small, tight ball.

And then it was Tuesday – a grey morning and mud on the water meadow – and no sign of Michael. In the form period, Manvinder came over and asked him to his party over Easter – 'Go and see a film before,' he said, smiling.

He wondered if they might have moved by then, imagining a hall filled with packing cases; car stuffed with clothes, pots and pans.

'Tony,' said Mr Rolph. 'Can you take the register back and drop in and have a chat with Miss Wilson?'

He looked up from his seat. Mr Rolph was staring across the room at him, his eyebrows raised in a question. He held up the register folder.

'Register?' he said. 'Miss Wilson?'

He got slowly to his feet. Everyone quiet and staring.

'Who's been a naughty boy then?' called Delaney, quickly adding: 'Just a joke, Mr Rolph. Nothing serious.'

'Not a joke, Steven. Not amusing.'

He picked up his bag, collected the blue folder and walked down the corridor, past E.13 – the Special Needs room – through the first set of fire doors and the cleaners' office, through the fire doors at the end, where he turned right and placed the register in the rack.

Michael hadn't turned up for school. On Monday, as he cycled home he'd wondered about Michael's meeting with the school authorities. Wondered whether he'd be able to be quiet long enough to get himself reinstated. Allowed back in.

And yet Tuesday had arrived and there was the empty space next to his. Mr Rolph had called his name out when he'd rattled through the register and had looked up when Michael hadn't answered, as if he was expecting the reply, 'Yes, sir.'

Miss Wilson's office was at the end of the main corridor, past the Sixth Form block and before the main assembly hall. Year 10 were shuffling in as he arrived.

The office door was slightly ajar and he could hear her voice on the phone. He stood for a moment, watching the students pushing and shoving their way through the two sets of doors. Mr Joseph, the Year Head, barking out warnings every few seconds, pulling people into line by their names: 'Humza Chaudhry. Just stop it. Yes. You. Behave yourself.'

Like a working dog, he thought, worrying away at wandering, disobedient sheep. Pushing and nudging them through the narrow gate.

Miss Wilson said: 'Bit of a disaster really. Yes. Carmell and myself . . . over in room 17. Only one case. Yes, yes . . . that's right . . .'

She was talking about a disciplinary interview, he realised. And Carmell, the governor – the owner of the building firm – was there to help decide whether a student should be allowed back into school. After they'd been chucked out. Tony moved closer to the door, watched as the last of Year 10 crept into the hall.

She was saying: 'Yes, yes, usual procedure. I simply explained what had gone on, during the field trip – that stuff with Delaney and Hudson . . .'

Mrs Stein walked past and climbed the stairs into the hall.

'Carmell went into his normal patronising act, you know: "Well, Michael, this isn't the first time you've appeared before me . . . " like he was some great judge in a criminal trial . . . I mean, quite honestly, I felt a sneaking sympathy with Slater whilst all this was going on . . . No, no that's not what caused the trouble, although I suppose it didn't help.

'It was while Carmell was going through the charges and so on, that Michael suddenly – yes, his mum was sitting there. I mean she gets smaller each time I see her. But when Carmell looked down to refer to some notes he'd made, Michael suddenly came out with: "You killed my dad." I mean, I thought he'd taken complete leave of his senses. You know, flipped his lid. Everything stopped; Carmell just gaped. Tried to speak – "Well, I, I—" – and Michael was straight back with, "You're the same Carmell of Carmell Construction, aren't you? The company that runs lorries with no brake lights. Kills innocent people?" '

Silence while she listened.

' . . . No really – I mean Michael was standing up, pointing and shouting. Banging on about how Carmell was destroying the wildlife at Ailsworth Heath. And then he simply turned to his mother and said, "That's it, Mum: I'm not staying here," and they were gone.'

There was the sound of a drawer opening in her

office, and then she began talking again.

'Carmell? Red-faced and wheezing like a great elephant seal.' And then: 'No, not a good idea.' She laughed. 'Probably Thursday evening.'

A few Year 10 stragglers ran past and tripped up the steps into the hall. He heard the receiver being replaced and he knocked lightly on the door.

A voice called: 'Come in.'

His absence letter was open on the table in front of Miss Wilson. On top of the brown folder that she'd used the last time he'd seen her. His personal file, he supposed.

She said: 'Tony, come and sit down.' And then, her left hand touching his letter, she said: 'You were ill on Friday?'

She looked at him carefully, her blue eyes clear and thoughtful. Did she want him to lie, he thought. To make his humiliation even worse when she went on to say, 'But I spoke to your mother yesterday afternoon, Tony – Monday? – and she said you were perfectly well . . .'

But his mother was at school yesterday. There couldn't have been a phone call.

He looked back at her. He said: 'I didn't feel too good, miss.'

'No, which is a pity because I wanted to have a chat

with you about the report card and how you thought you were getting on.'

'Right.' She didn't realise the letter was forged, he thought. That I simply tapped it out on the computer. Traced out the signature. Bundled it into an envelope. She's accepted the note as simply telling the truth.

The figure of the baby in the frame on the windowsill smiled back at him, but now it was almost as if he could share its pleasure, understand for the first time what it meant to have peace of mind. Like he'd just staggered in from some Geography field trip and he'd been able to slip a rucksack of hard rocks from his shoulders. He eased himself back into the chair.

'What do you think?'

And he realised that she'd asked him a question.

'I'm sorry?' he said.

And she smiled back thinly. 'I said, Tony, and do pay attention, I said: how do you think you got on last week?'

'Fine,' he replied. 'Except for Thursday.'

'Ah yes. Thursday. That was the day you got the weeks confused.'

'Yes, miss.'

'But you've got all the correct stuff for today – what is it?' – looking up at the timetable on her wall – 'English, History, Technology and Science?'

'Yes, miss.'

'So that next Tuesday, when we meet at half past three, you'll be able to say that everything is all right? That I can write a letter to your parents and confirm that you're no longer on the card?'

'Yes, miss.'

'So,' and again she looked at him with her clear blue eyes, 'perhaps you'd like to tell me about this tankard that Michael Slater is so excited about.'

Nineteen

Once, two years before, they'd gone to the Lake District.

'We need a spring break,' his father had said. 'You know, kick away the dark days of winter.' And so they'd booked a week in a cottage outside Keswick.

It was just after his father had finished at the shoe company and immediately before they'd started the magazine, before *Break Away* had come to squat on all their lives.

On the third day, they awoke to a blackbird playing its fountain of notes, and over breakfast, all sitting round a large map spread across the table, his father had suggested they bought a compass and took the tourist route up Great Gable.

'A proper mountain!' he'd said, laughing. 'We'll need to pack for the day,' and he'd gone off in the car to buy the compass, a walking stick and slabs of Kendal Mint Cake.

And yet, as he sat looking at Miss Wilson, the feeling of tension and pretence beginning to tighten his muscles and tug at his face, it had all ended in frustration and disappointment. They'd come down a narrow track to a gap between two parts of the mountain and his father, checking the map, had said: 'The summit is just up there,' – pointing to the great shoulder of rock rising up before them. 'Won't take us long now.'

But when they'd slogged their way up over stones and past boulders and against a wind that sucked their breath, with the horizon that always seemed to be treading a lighter step, and disappearing beyond the next pile of scree, they'd discovered that this wasn't the summit, and that there before them, in its different shades of brown, lay the great bulk of Great Gable, a full hour's upward climb. And so they'd sat on a rock and agreed that it was too long and too far and too difficult.

And now this about Michael and the tankard.

It was like Friday kept pulling him back into all the lies and deceit that surrounded the cycle ride to the heath. Sitting in Miss Wilson's office with his forged note carefully clipped to the file as though it was a genuine statement of fact.

'Oh,' he said. And then; 'I didn't know you'd seen Michael. What with him not being in school.'

She smiled, closing the folder, 'I saw him last evening. Had a chat with him and his mum before the disciplinary.'

'Oh,' he said again. 'Really.'

'Yes,' she said. 'Really. You want to smile more, Tony. You've got a great frown on your face as though you've committed some terrible crime. Lighten up!'

She leaned forward and pulled open a drawer in the steel filing cabinet, searching for the 'H's before making his folder disappear. She said: 'Michael Slater simply said that you and he had found some old tankard, or jug or something, and that you were trying to find out about it.'

'Yes,' he said, uncertainly, a smile hovering round his mouth like a wandering butterfly.

'I'm not trying to muscle in on your discovery or anything. It sounds fascinating.' And then: 'You could do an assembly on it, after Easter. I'm sure the Year group would be interested in something like that.'

And then the bell outside the door crashed through their conversation and she said, 'I'll see you at the end of the day, Tony,' and he'd got up and shouldered his bag, and walked off into the streets of Verona, in search of Romeo and Juliet.

Michael must have made the connection on the heath,

he thought. They'd stood there looking at the noticeboard and Michael had recognised the distinctive lettering of the name 'Carmell Construction'. He must have noticed the photograph as well: the grey hair and dark eyes looking out from beneath the silver birch.

Mr Rolph said: 'What is the point about Mercutio's death?'

He stood by the board, chalk between the fingers of his right hand, held down like a fresh-lit cigarette. Heads bent over books.

'Is it something to do with Romeo's er "relationship" with Juliet?' said Paul Garnett, working the syllables so that the sentence seemed to circle around the word 'relationship'. Like water rippling from a dropped stone.

'Ooh-missus!' said Delaney, flicking the hair from his face, dark eyes checking for laughter.

Tony leaned back and looked at the old dictionaries piled on the bookshelf by the blackboard. They were light blue and some had lost their covers, so the effect was like a stack of rock, with some of the strata badly eroded.

When they'd sat down to tea that last evening, his father had said, 'What do you think about Mr Eastman?'

and he realised that they were talking about the man from the estate agents.

His mother looked up from her plate of spaghetti, slowly turning the strands with her fork, like she was winding a clock. There was a dark line underneath her left eye which made her look tired. She said: 'I thought 95 sounded about right.'

And he understood that she was talking about the figure they might sell the house for. That '95' meant £95,000.

His father looked down at his meal. He said: 'Mmmm.'

'Did Mr Eastman like our house?' Tony asked. Wondering if the man, who he imagined as being old, wearing a brown jacket and carrying a notebook, had been interested in his bedroom, with its bookshelves and aircraft and posters and view out across the west side of town.

'He made the right noises,' his father said.

And his mother added, 'He was really here to measure the property – you know – find out how many rooms we've got, how big they are. That kind of thing.'

So he wouldn't have looked at their house as if it was 'someone', he thought, with its personality made by all of them sharing their lives. Those places that made their home different from others – the faded carpet in his parents' bedroom; the grey stain on the ceiling in the bathroom; the crack by the fireplace in the lounge that he always thought of as a river, twisting and turning as it bypassed the mantelpiece and curved out towards the TV before losing itself in the green folds of carpet, that spread like a sea.

'Will he help us find another house?' he said.

His parents looked at each other across the table, neither speaking, and in the silence he realised he'd stumbled upon something that was difficult, that they'd not sorted out or reached agreement over.

'Possibly,' his mother had said, and added: 'Now why don't you eat your tea before it gets cold?'

And this was the polite way of telling him to 'shut up'.

Later he stood next to his mother whilst she washed the dishes and he wiped them dry, staring out across the playing-field and wondering what new view they'd share in a few weeks' time. And so he said, 'Where will we live when we sell our house?' because he thought if he knew soon, then by the time they packed all their things away and said 'goodbye' to 220 Scotton Road, he would have got used to it, would have prepared himself for the change.

His mother stood still for a moment, leaning on

arms that disappeared beneath the grey surface of the washing-up water. Like she was trying to figure out an answer. Or maybe trying to imagine a different kind of life.

'Hard to say, Tony,' she said. 'It's going to be a bit smaller than this. We're going to look at a house on the other side of Drayton Park on Thursday evening. You can come too, if you like.'

He put a plate on the side, reached for another. He said: 'The new house will be – well – smaller – because, we're – we'll need to pay back some of the money? To the bank and everything?'

She placed a dish on the draining board. She said: 'Yes. You'll still have your own room and that. But, well,' looking down, ' – it won't be like this.'

'What do you think, Tony? Tony?'

'Toe-neeee,' said Steven Delaney through fingers that were curled over into a megaphone. 'Come in, Toe-neeee.'

'Sorry?' he said, realising that he'd been asked a question, the report card sitting on Rolph's table like a threat.

'I said, Tony,' said Mr Rolph, heavily underlining his name, 'what is the society like in Verona – in the play? How do people get on with each other? And Steven, keep your views to yourself. Unless you're asked for them. Quite clear?'

'Yes,' he said. 'Sir.'

'Right – Tony: Verona. What do you think?'

'It's, well' – he coughed. 'It was like Romeo and Juliet – they're like – on different teams. And that was what they were all born into. And no one seems able to talk about it. So there's fighting and that.'

'Mmm. "Fighting and that". What about his friend – Mercutio?'

'Well. That's just – you know: stupid. Doesn't make any sense.'

'"Doesn't make any sense"? Anyone?' said Mr Rolph, looking across the room.

Like Delaney and Michael, Tony thought. Senseless. Waste of time. Look where it got you. He put his hand up.

'Yes?' said Rolph.

'It's like people are born into the world and well – it's like dropping into the middle of a play. Everything's going on. Before they're around and – and—'

'What's he on about?' said Chris Phillips.

'Yer,' from Delaney. 'Been taking some of those dangerous chemicals I shouldn't wonder.'

'Quiet. What do you mean – like arriving "in the middle of a play"? That sounds interesting.'

'It's like we're all born into this world,' said Melanie Brookes behind. 'With all the rules and everything sorted out. Like in the play, the two families are rowing and fighting and the children just carry on. No one knows how to change anything.'

'And Mercutio gets killed?'

'Yes,' she said. 'Something like that.'

He thought of his room and the camouflaged flight turning slowly in the updraught of his opened door. And the view across the town and the shoebox of fossils stowed beneath the head of his bed.

It was like summoning a distant memory.

Twenty

He left school a shade before 3.40, just after the rain had started, so that by the time he arrived at Brighton Road, his trousers clung wetly to his legs. The rain blowing in freezing gusts and cascading off his jacket.

Michael's house overlooked the water meadow of the Scratch Brook, one of a group of three. Red-brick and sheltering behind an enormous privet hedge; a short drive that was occupied by an old white caravan.

When they were younger they had used the caravan as a hideout, and sometimes, when it was cold and wet during weekends, would settle inside and play board games or watch TV from the small portable set, Mrs Slater keeping them supplied with drinks and biscuits.

All that had stopped when Michael's father had been killed.

So it stood there, leaning slightly to one side because

of a flat tyre, and now old and bleached and bloated.

'Come in, Tony,' said Mrs Slater, holding the kitchen door back for him.

'Thanks,' he said. 'I'm soaked, I'm afraid. Got caught when the rain started.' He pulled off his backpack.

'You give me your jacket and I'll hang it up in the boiler cupboard,' she said. 'And really you could do with changing those trousers—'

'No, it's all right,' pulling an arm free from a wet sleeve.

'Michael!' called Mrs Slater, reaching for a coat hanger. 'Michael! — Tony's here. He's upstairs, Tony, would you like a cup of tea or anything?'

She was a short woman, only slightly taller than he was, and her face was long and thin, and whenever he called round and she was at home, she always seemed to be wearing a kind of overall on top of her clothes. A house coat his mother had told him; to protect clothes if housework was being done. Today she was dressed in a faded blue garment that was patterned with white flowers.

She had a kind of restlessness about her — like a sparrow or wren — so that once she'd hung his jacket in the cupboard, she was reaching for the kettle, and then crossing the kitchen to fetch the biscuit tin from the shelf. All the time talking with her soft Irish accent.

'We didn't do too well – at the disciplinary last night,' she said. 'Would you like a biscuit, Tony? That awful man – Carmell – was there, lording it over everyone. Coming straight to conclusions – without ever letting anyone consider the facts.'

'Oh,' he said.

'Take a seat, Tony,' and she followed him through the door into the small dining-room.

'A disgrace. I said that to Michael – last night – a complete disgrace. To assume that there's only one point of view and everything.'

She pushed back a strand of hair that had fallen across her face.

'Right,' he said, nibbling a biscuit.

'Of course, of course it didn't help matters – Michael having a go at him – but someone's got to stand up to these people.'

Behind her, on the sideboard, and wrapped like a mummy, bandaged in newspaper, was the tankard. It stood lopsidedly between a glass fruit bowl and a frame containing a picture of Mr Slater. Part of a headline was visible from where he sat: it said: 'Geni—'.

She saw him looking over her shoulder, gave a backwards glance and said: 'And then we've got this woman – this Mrs Wilberforce – dropping by. Heaven knows what she wants – with that old thing. I mean to

163

say – MICHAEL! – you can't think there's any value in it – surely?'

'It's pretty old, Mrs Slater,' he said, listening for signs of Michael's feet on the stairs.

'Yes, I can see that – Michael pointed out the date and everything – although he was pretty mysterious,' – her brown eyes focused on his face – 'about where you found it.'

'Right.'

'But I'm not going to pry – and anyway, there's the kettle,' – and she went back into the kitchen, going through into the hall to give Michael another shout.

'Well, boys,' said Mrs Wilberforce, 'what do you think we've got here?'

She looked across the small dining-table to where they sat, the tankard placed in the centre of its newspaper wrapping, tilted and shining greenly in the light.

'It's like a kind of drinking jug or something,' said Michael, his right hand reaching out and touching the roughened surface.

'Well, yes. Spot on,' and she pushed up her glasses, an old brown-rimmed pair that sat at an odd angle so it looked as if her eyes were planted like currants in a pile of dough. When she spoke several layers of flesh beneath her chin seemed to move together, and Tony thought of the great downturned mouth and bulk of an angler fish.

'But is it valuable?' he said.

'Yeah,' said Michael. 'Worth some money.' Flashing a grin.

'It has a history,' she said carefully, 'and before we can consider its monetary value, we would need to recover that history.'

'What's that mean?' said Michael. 'Like find out who it belonged to, stuff like that?'

She looked across the table to each of them, and breathing heavily said: 'There are two things of very great significance about your find. The first' – and she reached across the table and lifted the tankard, turning it slowly in the light – 'is this date that you can still see. And secondly, is the fact that you found it on Ailsworth Heath. Taken together the two facts could be of great significance.'

'Why's that then?' said Michael.

'I don't want to get too far ahead of myself,' she said. 'The first thing to do is to get it cleaned up so that we can have a proper look at what lies underneath. You spotted the date here,' – touching the place with a very clean forefinger – 'but why would anyone inscribe a date low down on the side of a tankard? What would be the point?'

They sat in the late afternoon of Michael's dining-room, hearing the shouts of children in the street outside; Mrs Slater pushing a vacuum cleaner around a bedroom overhead.

'It might have been presented to someone, for something they'd done. Like a prize,' Tony said, thinking of the FA Cup.

'Exactly!' said Mrs Wilberforce, her throat beginning to stir. 'I think this was given to someone for something they'd achieved; for something that was of – erm – great significance, and that it happened in 1820.'

'So, so are you going to put us out of our misery?' said Michael, his chin resting on his hands. 'Tell us the great secret?'

That was the thing with Michael, he thought, why he liked him: no messing around, get straight to the point. Mrs Wilberforce obviously knew more than she was letting on, had some kind of hunch. And yet she wasn't to be hurried. It was like watching someone think in slow motion – every word and phrase spooned out and weighed.

'When I leave here,' she said, 'I'm going to give you a task, get you involved in some research, that will take you down the library and maybe on to the internet, so that you can share with me the excitement of your find. But all in good time.'

She placed the tankard back on the newspaper. 'I would like to congratulate you for not attempting to clean the surface, because it would have been disastrous had you tried. I would – with your permission – like to take it back with me to Northampton and get it turned into something a little more presentable.'

'What's it made of?' Tony asked quietly, looking at the different shades of green and brown.

'I think,' said Mrs Wilberforce, 'that what you've got here is – probably, mind – a tankard made from copper that's been silver-plated. That would explain the rough, green surface. It's been tossed into fresh water and although the base rock at Ailsworth is limestone, the presence of decaying vegetation in the water – dead leaves and so forth – would have created very acidic conditions. The water would have acted like battery electrolyte. The copper would have corroded, and ironically, as it appeared on the surface, coating it so to speak, it would have protected the silver underneath and so preserved any inscription.'

'This sounds like a Science lesson,' said Michael. 'You're going to ask us to light our Bunsen burners any second, I can tell.'

'No, begone with you. This is far more interesting

than that. And the good thing for you both is that you can take part in finding out about it.'

This is like working with Mr King, he thought. When they'd found the fossils and had trotted round the front of the school to his office, covered in dust and with pockets stuffed with old shells, he'd said: 'Wow, what an amazing collection. We'll need to do some research to find out their names and when they lived.' He'd looked down at them, his mouth pulled into a smile.

Mrs Wilberforce seemed to be acting on a hunch – guesswork. Michael had said that when he'd mentioned the heath and the date on the phone she'd suddenly become interested. Like she knew something.

He could hear Mrs Slater next door spraying polish on the furniture. The hiss of the aerosol like the sigh of airbrakes. And he remembered the great lorry turning off the road when they'd made their cycle ride. The driver leaning out of his cab to ask for directions; daisies pressed down under the tread of the wheels.

'And so there we are,' Mrs Wilberforce said, touching the tankard tenderly. 'But before I go, and before I explain what I'd like you to do, let me tell you a story, something true that may help you appreciate the miracle of what you've found – that is, if my guess is correct.'

She settled herself in her chair, her blue eyes looking at each of them in turn. And each of them watching her in silence. They were aware that Mrs Slater stood at the doorway to the lounge, and that she too was listening.

'Once,' she said, 'there was a small boy. He was five years old and he lived in the countryside. His parents didn't have a lot of money and there were always too many mouths to feed. Each day the lad would look across at a nearby village, and watch the sun rise over the fields. And each day that same sun would cross the sky and disappear, beyond the trees, in the direction of another small settlement.

'The young lad, looking at the horizon of hedges and woods and fields, the countryside of swallows and badgers, wondered what there might be beyond – and whether that place might be the end of the world. And if you got there, got beyond the horizon, might you not be able to stand at the edge of the Earth and look out at the sun and stars and planets, all moving in their own way across the vastness of space?

'And so he pulled on his boots one bright morning in summer, and slipped out of the side door of the cottage without telling his mother what he was up to, and set out down the earth road in the direction of the midday sun. And he walked until he came to an area of open grassland, that hadn't been planted with crops, but just then sparkled with gorse and was tufted with heather and was bordered by a spreading wood of ancient broadleaf trees.

'And there he stopped because as far as he walked, so the horizon seemed to get further and further away. But he didn't forget the place or the day he'd set out in search of the end of the world. And when he was older and was able, he wrote about it and about other visits he made down that same earth track. And the place those five-year-old legs trudged to was Ailsworth Heath.'

Tony thought of the small boy and the yellow road. No sound of contractors then. No fences or chainsaws. Sunk in the smell of flowers and the sound of insect wings; birdsong and the dark spikes of green gorse.

'He was a writer, then?' he asked.

'Go into the town library, near the museum, and find the poetry section,' she said. 'And if you're lucky you'll find some books written by John Clare.'

'And he's famous and everything?' said Michael. 'Mr Rolph would have heard of him?'

'Mr Rolph's your teacher? Well, then, I'm sure Mr Rolph would have heard of John Clare – the great writer who once went off in search of the edge of the world.'

'And lifted that tankard – those years ago? In some old pub?'

'I think so,' she said. 'Yes.'

Twenty-one

'Something you picked up, last week – on that field trip of yours?' Mrs Slater had said, after Mrs Wilberforce had placed the tankard in a case and walked out to her car. 'I don't know why you didn't mention it earlier – instead of being all mysterious – and saying you "just found it" – I bet that Mr Jordan would have been interested had you shown him – at the time – might have saved us all a lot of bother. Eh, Michael?'

'Yes, Mum,' he said.

'You're not stopping for tea then, Tony? I can't tempt you with fish fingers and chips?'

'No, no – I'll have to be going,' he said, putting an arm into the sleeve of his jacket. 'Thanks.'

'We'll be back on the phone – in a week or two's time,' she said, turning on the hot water tap. 'I've been promoted to supervisor – at the station – so we thought we'd get ourselves sorted – with the phone company.'

'Oh,' he said. 'Good.' And then; 'Thanks for the tea and biscuits.'

Michael followed him out to where his bike was parked, anchored to the side of the caravan.

'Not something you can really mention to your folks,' Michael said. 'Our tankard. Not unless you alter the Ailsworth part. Turn it into Tuesday rather than last Friday.'

'Yes,' he said. One set of lies breeding another. Friday was now Tuesday. The visit to Michael to see Mrs Wilberforce was really staying after school to attend a computer club.

'Seems a bit odd,' said Michael, 'the tankard no longer lodging safe and sound here. I hope the old bat looks after it.'

She'd said that it would have to be soaked in a 30 per cent solution of formic acid. 'That will remove the copper corrosive products and should enable us to see what might be written above the date,' she'd said, carefully pushing together the newspaper.

'So, this John Clare was a poet?' he'd asked.

And when she'd nodded, he'd said: 'But how do you know the tankard might have belonged to him? It could have been anyone, surely?'

'What a good questioner you are,' she said, smiling. 'The two things I mentioned when I arrived: firstly, the location of your find was a pond two or three miles south of Helpston; secondly, the date on the tankard is 1820. Both of these point, irresistibly, I would say, towards only one owner, and that's Clare. More I'd rather not say until we've got it cleaned up,' and she lifted her case on to the table and flicked a catch so that its mouth opened like the jaws of some predatory fish. 'What you might like to do, to help establish the background, help confirm my theory, is to go down the library – in town or at school – and see what you can find out. The internet will be a help.'

And with that she snapped the lock on the case and said: 'This is most exciting. And I'm pleased that you picked up the phone last Saturday. Goodbye!'

'I'll have to be getting back, Michael,' he said, and then, as an afterthought, 'When will you be coming to school?'

Michael looked down and kicked a stone into the hedge. 'As soon as they've put together a new judge and jury, mate. This week. Thursday or Friday? Don't like to keep you hanging around. I might wait for you, over in the park.'

★ ★ ★

He left Brighton Road at ten to six and pedalled up the hill towards Weston Lane. Along past the row of lime trees with the view of Gretford stretching away to his left, like a great patterned carpet.

Mrs Wilberforce had said she would need to keep the tankard for the rest of the week but that she might be contacting them on Thursday evening.

'It will need to be soaked in solution for a day or so,' she said. 'And then I'll report back on what I've found and advise you on what you should do.'

The wind on the hill made the great trees sound like breakers on the sea and he bent his head once more and pushed down, watching the ground pass in a grey stream. Up ahead the rooks turned slowly, their great *craaw-craaw* scouring the sky. It was like early November, he thought, with the days short and the winter dark ahead.

What would he say to his parents – about Mrs Wilberforce and their find? What script would he read from? Because before she'd gone, he'd given her his phone number as the point of contact. So that when she phoned, say Thursday evening, and his father lifted the receiver, after a day at the printers trying to get the last issue of the magazine straight, he'd want to know exactly who Mrs Wilberforce from the county museum might be and what she had to do with phoning his son on a Thursday evening.

'What was the computer club like?' his mother asked. She was sitting in the alcove with a pile of page proofs from the magazine. Checking for errors.

'Fine,' he said. 'Where's Dad?'

'Dining-room. Bashing through late ads.'

'Oh.' And he briefly wondered whether that meant they'd have enough to pay back the money that was owed. So that they wouldn't have to move. But then again, there was a pile of 'houses for sale' sheets stacked by the bread bin, so perhaps not.

'I'm a bit tied up with these,' his mother said, pointing to the pages in front of her. 'Do you think you could sort yourself out some tea? There's a lasagne in the freezer if you want to bung that in the microwave.'

'Yes,' he said, and looked in the food cupboard.

He could hear his father tapping away in the dining-room, the flurry of clicks like the passing of a goods train at the station. When he stopped Tony could imagine him leaning into the screen, moving about pieces of text with the mouse, finger poised, ready to click bits of design into place.

Sometimes, with less than forty-eight hours to go before taking the magazine to the printers, his father would work through the night and then on into the next day. The problem with the late adverts was that they often came with strings attached. He remembered his father explaining, on their second issue, that two of the larger adverts required 'editorial support'.

'What's that?' he'd said, imagining some kind of scaffolding being put into place.

'Well, look here' – and he'd shown him a frame that promised 'High quality meals at low cost prices'. 'See,' he said, 'the George Inn at Calderhay have bought this space, but they want us to write something nice about the pub in our "Away Days" section. So I'll give them a couple of paragraphs that explains to the reader that a good place to stop for a decent meal will be the pub.'

And he'd nodded and his father had gone back to work and he'd walked away, feeling that somewhere things weren't quite right, because if people read articles on interesting places to go, they wouldn't want to read advice that was paid for by some company or other. They'd expect an honest opinion. If the George Inn was OK you could say so but not because there were hundreds of pounds sticking to each letter and full stop.

'Remove the sleeve. Perforate the film cover and microwave on full power for 8 minutes,' he read.

Back at the table, his eye fell on the school newsletter: *Contact*. There was an advert on the front for a computer course. He turned the page. Inside there was

177

another – a box explaining you could prepare for your holidays by learning French at the school. A ten-week course for £120. It was like Dad's magazine. He could imagine that soon they'd be going to school with the names of companies printed on their sweatshirts. Like footballers.

Later, as he sat stirring a strawberry yoghurt, his father came into the kitchen. His face was grey and Tony noticed that he hadn't shaved that morning. Bits of stubble caught the light and shone like silver splinters.

'Good day?' his father said, letting water into the kettle.

'OK.' And then; 'How is the magazine?'

'Terrible,' and his father made a face. 'The computer hasn't been behaving itself.'

'What – our one, you mean?'

'That's it – Rebecca, how are you getting on?'

And he'd gone to where his mother was working through the completed pages. She had a list of corrections she'd been making in her notebook.

'Just odd things,' she'd said. 'A couple of words missed out and on this one – for Gretford Pool – there's no contact phone number.'

'We're not going to do it at this rate,' his father said. And then: 'We're running out of nights if we're to get this lot to the printers.' He pushed his fingers through his hair, the spaces beneath his eyes thrown into shadow.

Tony looked down. Scanned the words on the yogurt pot: '3.8 grammes of protein,' he read. '13.1 grammes of carbohydrate.' If they missed the Thursday print deadline then the magazine would be late. And the advertisers might want their money back. And that meant they'd have to pay for the magazine themselves. Out of money they didn't have.

His mother said: 'Take a seat, David, and I'll make the tea. And don't worry – there are two of us in this thing.'

'Oh, I know,' he said. 'I know,' rubbing his hand over his face. 'But I'm tired and – and – I just wonder how much more of this we can take.'

Twenty-two

'Beautiful property, Mrs Hudson – or may I call you Rebecca? Wonderful view from up here. Plenty of room for development,' – and a great hand, covered in bristly dark hair reached out and clutched the cotton holding his squadron in place. The aircraft collapsed into each other, pieces of propeller dropping on to his bed.

'You've got to make good use of surface area. You know that, don't you, Master Hudson? You know that's important.' A huge face, like a slab of granite, leaned into his own; small grey eyes, stinking breath.

'Answer Mr Carmell,' said a voice. It was his mother. She was standing in the dark, by the door. Holding her hands together, like she was anxious.

'Yes,' said Carmell. 'You know what's important,' – raising aloft the wrecked aircraft, like a bunch of severed hands.

He awoke in sweat, the duvet trapping him in its

turns and folds. He pulled at the material, freed himself, and sat up. He'd left his curtains partly open and fresh white light flooded in from the garden, dripped across his desk, pooled on the floor by the door.

It was just after 2.20 and there was no sound from his parents' room. No sound of fingers on plastic tapping away downstairs.

After his father's outburst, he had walked quietly across the kitchen and dropped the yoghurt pot into the bin; had made his way upstairs and spent the rest of the evening completing a map for Geography.

'OK?' his mother had asked as he lay in bed.

'Yes,' he'd said. 'I'm pretty fine.' And then, not really knowing what to say: 'And how is Dad?'

She looked back, over her shoulder, listening as if he might hear. She said: 'He's very busy – and – well – what with everything else – he's a bit wound up. But he'll recover.' Pause in the half-light of his lamp: 'We all will.'

That next morning, after he'd stirred some breakfast cereal around his plate, he'd got his mother to check and sign his report card and then had gone out to fetch his bike from the shed. He didn't need to make a close inspection of the rear wheel to see that the tyre was flat. The kind of flat that meant it wasn't a slow puncture

181

and so that he'd need to collect the levers from the kitchen drawer and the glue and patches and chalk and sandpaper and remove and repair the inner tube. It was just turning 8.25.

His mother said: 'Look, I don't have to be at Stratford until nine. I'll give you a lift.'

And later still, as she turned the car in the direction of Beech Farm Road, and they passed straggling groups of students walking towards Crichton College, he suddenly said: 'I didn't go to school last Friday.'

She glanced down at him, alarm flashing across her face. And then, as she stopped by the school crossing, said: 'What happened?'

He hadn't really been planning to say anything, but it was like being trapped by the duvet, he felt that he simply couldn't carry on, with the way the lies were multiplying. Things were getting so complicated he was beginning to lose track of where he said he'd been or what he said he'd been doing. Whatever the consequences and however difficult he found the explanation, he needed to be able to say to someone, 'This is what happened. That's all there is to it.'

And so, as the car swung left and then right up Weston Hill, he'd explained what really had taken place during their field trip, how they'd been pushed into the pond and how they'd got the blame for Delaney's actions. How they'd decided to ride back to Ailsworth Heath on Friday because there didn't seem to be any other way of recovering the tankard that they'd seen.

'You cycled all that way?' she said, pulling on to the verge near the old windpump on Weston Lane.

'Yes,' he said, 'it took a few hours. A policeman gave us a lift back.'

'And – well, did you find what you were looking for?'

'Oh. Yes – yes,' he said, realising from her response that she wasn't simply going to sit there and give him the cold treatment. Using his hands to explain: 'Michael waded in and brought back this greeny sort of tankard. It doesn't look like much but – well – this woman, from the museum in Northampton? – well, this woman, she says it probably belonged to this really famous poet. John Clare. And – well – she's taken it with her to get it cleaned up and everything and she'll then be able to tell us about it.'

He looked away, through the windscreen, where drops of rain were beginning to fleck the glass. A pair of blackbirds raced across the road. He listened for his mother's response.

'I don't know what to say,' she said at last, looking down at her hands folded below the steering wheel. 'It would have been so much easier had you been able to

183

tell us about the Delaney business from the start – we could have seen Miss Wilson and got it sorted out.'

'Nothing you could have done,' he said. 'About Delaney.'

'This isn't the Mafia,' she said, suddenly angry. 'This code of silence is stupid. You could have got yourselves killed – on the crazy bike ride. Both of you.' And then, her voice suddenly calm: 'Does Michael's mum know anything about this?'

'Not about Friday. But this woman from the museum, Mrs Wilberforce, called in to his house last night.'

'When you were at your "computer club"?'

'Yes,' he said, looking down.

They sat gazing out over the fields, seeing the sky pulled into tufts by the wind that rocked the car every few minutes.

'And that's it, Tony?' his mother said. 'There's no more?'

He didn't meet her gaze. 'There's absolutely nothing else.' And then he remembered the absence note. 'Except—'

'Yes?' she said.

'I typed out a note, for Mr Rolph. When you and Dad went looking at houses. On Sunday.'

'Right. I can see you might need to do something like that.' She pushed her hair away from her face and turned towards him. 'The trouble is once you start saying one thing and well—'

'— doing something else?'

'Yes. Life gets really complicated. You end up not knowing what you've said to people. And where you said you'd been.'

'I know,' he said quietly.

'I'm glad you told me,' she said, touching his arm. 'But – well, what with the magazine and that – you know – I won't explain everything to your dad, at the moment.'

'Yes,' he said.

'There's nothing you want me to do? I can't come into school – have a quiet chat with Miss Wilson? About Steven Delaney?'

'No, thanks. But – on Thursday – tomorrow – the woman from the museum, Mrs Wilberforce, will be phoning. To let us know what she's found out – about the tankard.'

'OK.' She turned the key in the ignition. 'Your father will probably be out at the printers.'

He waited for Quest to settle down, with all the graphics and adverts in place. Moved the cursor over to the search box and typed in 'John Clare'; clicked the action button.

The screen cleared for several seconds and then the message: '*Matched 1 of 1*'.

He looked down:

Payne, John: A Dictionary of Renewable Resources.

Clare's first name had been matched but there was nothing else.

He scrolled to the bottom of the page, clicked on Fusion and waited for the results of the next search.

It was 12.20 and the library was filling up: Year 7 students coming in out of the rain; sixth formers with their large black files; Mrs Kaur with a group from her Year 8 class.

'Downloading some porn, then?' said Delaney in his ear. Spanier coming into view at his side, grinning. 'Still without your little mate, then?'

'Get lost, Delaney,' he said to himself. 'Go and take a walk.'

The screen cleared and three pairs of eyes read from the list of matched headings:

John Clare: A Reader's Guide (T L Peters and S Rayburne, 1976)

John Clare: Poetry in the Age of the Romantics (A R Brooks, 1998)

Sanity and Madness in the Poetry of John Clare (M Forester, 1993).

'Phwoar!' said Delaney, nudging his chair. 'This is a

bit strong, eh mate? John Clare – the poet. Phwoar!' he said again. 'Getting a bit serious, eh, Antonio? Boffing into the library and looking up poetry on the internet.'

Mrs Kaur was busy in the Drama section; her face was turned away from them. The librarian was using the photocopier.

'Must fancy himself,' said Spanier. 'But that's not surprising – nobody else does.'

'Not if he's into reading "poetry",' said Delaney, laughter about his cold eyes. When he said 'poetry' his voice changed pitch, pushing the first syllable, so that it sounded like the speech of someone from Crichton House.

'Yeah,' Tony said, clicking on the 'reader's guide'. 'Thanks for showing an interest.' Knowing that he had to keep looking at the screen.

He felt rather than saw Delaney's fist stab into his arm. 'Don't push your luck, mate,' he hissed, warm breath against his neck. 'Else you might not make it when you're pedalling home. C'mon, Span – let's leave this jerk to his pathetic "poetry".'

'See you later, "Antonio",' said Spanier, roughing his hair as he went past.

They mooched out of the library, laughing, Delaney stretching out a hand as they passed the counter and brushing a stack of leaflets on to the floor. More laughter. And then they were gone, racing each other down the corridor.

He looked at the screen for a full minute. Waited for his breathing to get back to normal; for the ache to drop from his shoulders.

'Need any help, dear?' said Mrs Johnson, the librarian, coming across to where he sat.

'No,' he said. 'No, thanks. Just thinking.'

He called up a list of key dates from Clare's life, but when they appeared, with the years over on the left-hand side and single lines explaining what had taken place, it was difficult to get a feel for what the man was like. And yet there were important clues if you were patient.

1793: Born in Helpston, it said.

Was that why Mrs Wilberforce had linked the tankard with the poet? But surely there had to be more than that? Thousands of people must have lived there, over the years. She must know something else. He thought back to the thatched roofs, the flowers and posters in the windows. Where they'd wandered with their worksheets. Before the episode of the pool. Before the report card. Before Michael had been thrown out. Jordan hadn't bothered with a question about the poet. Probably didn't know.

He scrolled down, the life rushing past like scenery

on a train. He'd worked as a potboy in a pub, as a gardener and as a labourer.

That didn't seem to be the kind of work a poet might do, imagining a man sitting in a loft, a feathered quill touching his lips while he put together important thoughts.

But a labourer? Someone digging ditches and whacking in fence posts?

1820, it said, *publication of Poems Descriptive of Rural Life and Scenery*. His first book.

'1820' they'd read on the tankard, the faint letters tilted to the right. The find in the pond and pages of poetry – linked 180 years ago?

Mrs Stein came into the library. She was asking at the desk about a CD-Rom.

He thought of the celebration assembly and the endless queue of students trooping up to collect their certificates, for good attendance and excellent work. Was the tankard something like that? A prize for a poor man who had written a book?

He pressed the scroll bar, watching the important dates, the many children born into the Clare family, blur past and then crashed into:

1864, 20 May. Dies at Northampton Asylum.

And that was it. There was nothing else. Just dies at the asylum.

Over on the other side of the library, Mrs Kaur said: 'You'll find plenty of stuff for your project on these two shelves. Just ask at the desk if you've got a problem.'

Wasn't an asylum the place where people who were mentally ill were kept, like a hospital, he wondered. Was that what happened to Clare? The famous poet who was mentally ill? And had to be locked away? But that wouldn't explain, surely, why the tankard had ended up amongst the pondweed and leaf-mould?

Who had been responsible for that?

He went back to the submenu and clicked on 'works'. It was 12.38 on the library clock. He selected a poem about a skylark, looked at its long lines and tried to make sense of the knots of words spreading across the screen, stumbling over the beginning until he fetched up against:

> *'Above the russet clods the corn is seen*
> *Sprouting its spirey points of tender green*
> *Where squats the hare to terrors wide awake*
> *Like some brown clod the harrows failed to break'*

'Russet' was strange, but 'clods' – bits of earth? And the corn – he'd seen fields in November planted with wheat, like lines of new grass. Like 'spires' in fact. 'Spirey', like the great rocket point of Gretford Church. Each shoot of corn was like a spire – and amongst all of

190

this was a hare – 'to terrors wide awake'. Alert, scared – looking out for danger.

It was like watching a nature programme, he thought. But better, because you had to puzzle away at the language, work to make it give up its secret. And not worry too much if you weren't that sure of some of the strange expressions you stubbed your toe against.

He clicked the print button and waited for the inkjet to pass the paper through its rollers, wondering whether the young man who had the sharp eye for words was that same young man who had grasped the tankard they had pulled, green and dripping, from the grey waters of the old heath.

Twenty-three

Sunday 2 April   A discovery
We'd found this old drinking mug in a pond, Michael and me.
It doesn't look that exciting, being all green and dented but
there's a place where you can see a date – that's 1820. When
we found it we went to the museum in Gretford, but
they didn't know what it was, but Mrs Wilberforce from
Northampton came and took it away with her. She said she
thought it might belong to this famous poet. His name is John
Clare.

I looked him up on the internet last Wednesday. He wrote
this poem about the countryside. He described a hare hiding in
a ploughed field. Like it was terified of people.

On Saturday Mrs Wilberforce came and visited us at
Michael's house. She said the tankard definately belonged to
the poet although we'd have to wait until a court could
decide whether we might keep it. She said Northampton or
Peterborough museum would like to put the tankard on show.

On the other side of the classroom he could hear the rain spitting against the window, like someone chucking handfuls of small stones at the glass. 8.44 by the clock above Rolph's head. Tuesday of the last full week before the Easter break. Completing English homework in registration.

There was that other thing as well, that Mrs Wilberforce had said. He picked up his pen:

The museum has issued a press release which is like a letter that goes to newspapers and TV companies, explaining about the tankard and everything. They might want to talk to us about it and we could find ourselves on local television or radio.

Not that his father had been that excited – not after Mum had explained to him about the tankard and how they'd got it. 'Telling us a pack of lies,' he'd shouted. 'Taking a day off school – and with the Slater boy.'

'It's OK, David. I've talked to him about it. It's all right.' Holding his arm, calming him down.

'But you simply can't go playing fast and loose like that,' he said.

'I know, David, I know. But we're all a bit stressed at the moment. I'll make you some tea. Things will look a bit more reasonable then.' Holding on to him so that he wasn't frightening any more. No longer the runaway car. Pushing him into his chair at the table.

And during the remainder of Sunday afternoon, when his father came out of the dining-room, face a mass of bristles, and smudges beneath his eyes, he'd looked at Tony, working on his homework in the alcove, like he didn't quite know what to make of the situation any more.

Tony started to count the number of words he'd written when he heard a click and the classroom door opened: Michael entered, accompanied by Miss Wilson.

'Slay-ter, Slay-ter,' began Kevin Douglas, until frozen by a look from the Year Head. 'You can return to your place, Michael,' she said.

And with a slight grin, Michael wandered down the aisle and slid into the seat next to Tony's. Michael said: 'Bit of a surprise – eh?'

'Yeah.'

'How did you get on – at the – you know—?'

'Disciplinary? – 's OK. Report card until the end of term. Keep out of trouble until Easter. That kind of touch. Heavy if there's another – er – "incident".' He looked down. And then: 'Said it was a "final warning". No coming back if anything happens again.'

'It's good to see you, Michael,' said Rolph, after Miss Wilson had gone. Smiling across the rows of tables.

'Speak for yourself,' said Delaney, leaning back in his chair and staring at the ceiling.

'You spoke, Steven?' asked Rolph. Placing an extra pause between 'spoke' and 'Steven'. Like there was a threat in the half-second gap between the two words.

'Noth-ing,' said Delaney. 'Just glad to see the swimming champion back.'

Rolph let the laughter ripple round the room and then the bell went and they collected their bags and shuffled towards the door.

Rolph said: 'Could I see you for a moment, Michael?'

And so Tony waited outside, in the filling corridor, while his friend stood listening as Rolph told him to ignore Delaney and anyone else and to keep his head down for the remaining days until the Easter holiday.

And then they'd walked off to the Maths block, past the toilets and the hall and the library, past the corridor that led down towards Humanities and then the stairs beside the entrance to Science. And as they walked he wondered whether teachers ever considered what they meant when they made statements or recommended courses of action.

'Keep out of trouble,' said Mr Rolph to Michael. 'Keep out of trouble.' But at Scratch Brook, trouble wasn't waiting around like a puddle in the side of the road, or pieces of broken glass on the pavement; trouble was the stuff that came rushing at you without warning, that landed a fist in your face when you were busy thinking about something else. Trouble was the persistent tap on the shoulder whilst you were waiting in the dinner queue, library books stuffed into your bag by someone else, the missing PE kit. Trouble was a 'doing' word, he thought. A verb.

They arrived outside M3 and Michael wandered down the corridor, black bag slung over his shoulder, as he went off to find his own small-set Maths group. And Tony tagged on to the end of the queue that rippled out and back as though it were some giant, exotic millipede. Delaney over on the other side, leaning against the window ledge, chatting to James Hargreaves, eyes flicking across the different faces.

And after an hour of equations, that spread across his page like a field of thistles, it was back into the jostling crowd of the stairs and the push on to History, Mrs Roberts standing at the open door and yelling down the corridor: 'Do not run,' as Kevin Douglas raced to beat Manvinder Tethi.

'Now. Wait here properly,' said Roberts. 'In a straight line. Without a sound.'

In a straight line; without a sound – like the piece of paper, the tightly screwed ball, that skidded through the air and struck the side of Michael's head, not ten minutes later, as they struggled to make sense of the canal age in the 19th century.

Michael sat up, a faint red stain spreading across his face. He looked across to where Delaney saluted with a forefinger, a thin smile marking his face like a scar.

And he slowly got to his feet, and walked over to where the ball had landed in the aisle between the rows of tables, and he said to Mrs Roberts: 'Excuse me, miss, could I just go and return this to Steven Delaney?' And he opened his hand and showed her the screwed-up ball. 'After all, miss,' looking out over the class, 'it might be something important. Like his brain.'

'Let's be sensible,' she said, to the great roar of laughter. 'Go and put the paper in the bin. And you – Steven Delaney. I would like to see you at the end of the lesson. You'd better make sure that your work is up to scratch. Is that quite clear?'

'Anything you say, Mrs Roberts,' said Delaney, slouching back in his chair, right arm stretched out to the pen that doodled over his jotter.

'And I don't want to hear from you again until the bell goes.'

But then there was a knock at the door and when the Year 7 girl came in, looking nervously to her right, she said, 'Excuse me, Mrs Roberts, but Mrs Stein would like to see Michael Slater and Tony Hudson.'

Twenty-four

She looked up from her desk and smiled. She said: 'Ah, Tony and Michael. From 9JR.'

And she got up and walked over to where they were standing.

'You're not in trouble if that's what you're thinking,' looking at Tony. 'No, this is much more pleasant. Would you like to take a seat?' and she pointed to the chairs grouped around a small octagonal table.

'Can I get you anything to drink?' she said. 'We've probably got some squash in the office.'

But they looked at each other and then said that they were all right, so Mrs Stein turned to her desk and lifted a notebook and her diary and a blue fountain pen and came back and joined them.

The office wasn't particularly big, he thought. Probably about the same space as his bedroom. But there were hundreds of books on shelves against two of the walls. Hardbacks mainly, that seemed to be about literature – Shakespeare and Dickens and other writers he didn't recognise.

Michael said: 'It's like a cliff. The books.'

And she sat down and smiled. 'Yes. There are a lot. I'm a bit of a hoarder. I've always had difficulty in throwing out books, even if they're not on something I particularly care about.'

He understood that. He hadn't really liked the model he'd once been given of the Blackburn Beverley – a military transport aircraft that looked like some tropical snake that had just swallowed a pig – huge and bloated – the fuselage suspended on slender wings and powered by four tiny engines. And yet there it was, dwarfing his planes in its bulk, but flying straight and level next door to the stripped-down beauty of the Mustang.

Mrs Stein seated herself opposite them, placing her books and pen on the coffee table. She smiled and said: 'I've taken you from your lesson because of a phone call I received not five minutes ago.'

She paused and looked at each of them, like she wanted to see the effect her announcement would have on their faces.

'Really,' Tony said, not liking the silence and feeling it was only polite to say something.

'Yes,' she said. 'Colin Doyle from Midlands TV would like you both to go to Ailsworth Heath, tomorrow morning, and be interviewed about the tankard that you found. Ten days ago.'

'Television,' he said stupidly.

'Yes. He said that a Mrs Wilberforce – is that right? – had established – found out – that the tankard belonged to the poet John Clare?'

'That's right,' he said. Wondering whether she would ask them when they'd been over to the heath to find the tankard. And might it have been on that same occasion when he'd been away from school.

But Michael said: 'And we wouldn't be paid or anything? Not like a fee or something?'

'No,' said Mrs Stein. 'Nothing like that, I'm afraid. Mrs Wilberforce will pick you up from here. At a quarter to eleven. So there are some compensations.' She paused, letting the news take effect. She said: 'You'll have to tell me how you found the tankard and the research you completed. Fill me in.' She flipped open the cover of her notebook and turned to a fresh page. 'Where did you find it?' she asked, smiling.

It wasn't just politeness, or curiosity, he thought, as they took it in turns to retrace their steps to the heath and explained how they'd recovered the tankard and how Mrs Wilberforce had become involved. She wouldn't be taking notes, he thought, if it was simply politeness. You only make notes if you needed the information for something else.

In English, Mr Rolph, standing by the blackboard, had said: 'There's no point, boys and girls, in setting out to make notes – from a book or a lesson – unless you've worked out in advance what you need the information for. Is it to help give a talk? Answer questions? Prepare for a test? Win the National Lottery?'

They'd laughed, he remembered.

And so, when they'd finished and she'd said, 'What I'd like to do, with your exciting news, is to tell the *Gretford Mercury* about your discovery,' he thought, she must have been jotting down points to help her discussion with the paper.

And it was like finding something else about the adult world. Something he'd stumbled upon. Like there were different versions of people. There was the Mrs Stein who'd been cold and difficult when he was picking litter out by the rose bushes at the front of the school, and here there was this friendly person who'd taken them out of their class and had offered them squash and was really interested in their story.

And yet it wasn't that exactly, he thought later, lying on his back and staring once more at the way the light bounced off the rivets and stretched metal of his squadron. It was like she'd heard the story from the television company and had thought that the local paper might also want to carry the news. And that they'd be interviewed and later photographed outside their classroom.

But what story would get heard? Would it be about Michael Slater and Tony Hudson and what they'd gone through to find the tankard? Or would it simply be a nice picture and more success for Scratch Brook school?

He looked across at his noticeboard and at the old photograph. This wasn't like finding the pile of fossils, he thought. That world seemed as faded as the yellow news cutting. A distant dream.

But then the bell for break sounded and so they'd got up and walked to the door and passed, like minnows through a net, into the secretary's office and then out on to the main corridor.

After all the interest and conversation caused by Mrs Stein's news, and the questions from Mr Rolph in registration and Mr Travis in Technology, they'd trudged through the afternoon, met on the Year 7 playground, outside the library, and headed for the cycle sheds.

Where Delaney, with a piece of grass sticking out of the corner of his mouth, lolled against an upright; Spanier astride one of the bikes.

'So you're going to be in the news,' Delaney said, taking the grass out of his mouth and flicking it away, like a discarded cigarette.

'Maybe,' said Michael, feeling in his pocket for the key to his lock.

'Pair of film stars,' Spanier sneered, looking over the ranks of bikes.

'Nar,' said Delaney. 'Film stars have to remember their lines: Slater there can hardly write his name.'

In the silence, as Tony loosed his backpack, he could hear the wind hissing against the metal of the stands; the grass on the field curled like ripples on a beach.

Michael dropped his bag and walked deliberately to where Delaney leaned, his arms now crossed.

'What's the matter with you? You go looking for fist or something, mate?' Michael said, pushing his knuckles under the chin of the other.

'Just having a laugh, Michael,' he said, shoving the hand away. 'Thought you might like to show me and Span the famous mug everyone is excited about.' He laughed. 'We're real fans of poetry, me and Span.'

But as he turned, so Michael seized his arm and snatched him back; grabbing his collar by the throat and pulling his face close. 'Don't mess about, Delaney,' he said. 'This – all of this stuff that you do, it's pointless.

Stupid. I'm on a final warning – but don't push me again.'

'Oh, yeah,' said Delaney, tugging himself clear and straightening his sweatshirt. 'Or else?'

'Or else you'll make it worth my while.'

'I don't think we want to make it worth anyone's while,' said a smooth voice, and standing there, in his black coat and slicked-back hair, was Carmell, a document case in his hand and a frown across his face.

'You're the student I saw a week ago. At the disciplinary hearing. Michael Slater. That's right, isn't it?' he said.

'Something like that,' said Michael. 'And you're the git who kills innocent people. That's also right, isn't it?'

And he turned and collected his bike from the rack, stretched his leg over the crossbar and cycled down the slope towards Furnace Lane.

Twenty-five

6th April   A surprise

Sometimes you're so full of excitment that you feel you're going to burst, like when it's the last day of the summer term and you've left school and there's weeks and weeks of freedom rolling out ahead. I felt like that yesterday. The sky was realy clear and everything smelt clean and fresh. I'd spent most of the morning at Ailsworth heath with Michael Slater. We'd been intervewed by Midlands tv about this tankard we'd found in a pond. As everyone now knows – well most people at my school, it belonged to this realy famous poet, John Clare.

So I was pelting home to tell my mum and dad about the day – about what it was like to answer questions into a microphone and stare into a camera and I also wanted to get the tv switched on – so I could see what I looked like when the local news started.

And yet it wasn't like that. I charged down Windsor, the steep hill near to where we live, turned left at the botom, and it was like – like someone had just booted me in the stomache

*or socked a fist into my face, because there was this sign
outside the house, sticking out from near the holly bush. It
was bright red and it had the words 'For Sale' printed in
large, black letters. Like the flag of an army that had just
walked in.*

*Everything was normal in the morning when I left – I
didn't really notice our small pond, the old grave of my guinepig
– but now, with the sign, it was like my home belonged to
someone else.*

The day had been knifed down the middle: carved into
'before' and – there was no word to describe 'after'. Just
a feeling – cold and empty and dark.

On the heath they'd watched this woman, Millicent
Jones, looking at her face in a small mirror, tugging at
some loose strands of hair and then on a single 'OK' to
the cameraman, she had said: 'Well, boys, here we are in
the middle of an expanse of heathland, just west of
Peterborough, and you two made an exciting discovery
about ten days ago. Tell me what happened.'

'We were on a school trip,' Michael said, 'from
Gretford. And when we stopped for lunch me and
Tony wandered over to this pool. You know – to have a
look and that. And while we were checking the water,
we saw this sort of dark shadow – under the surface –
we tried to get it out.'

'But you weren't successful on that first occasion. Why was that?'

They looked at each other and Tony said: 'There was a bit of an accident—'

'– and we both got a soaking—'

'But you were so interested in what you'd spotted that you cycled almost thirty miles from your homes to see if you could retrieve what you'd found?'

'Yeah,' Michael said, grinning. 'It was a bit of a hard 'un. Backbreaking and that. But we got here all right.'

'And Michael rolled up his jeans and waded—'

'– and we got a grip of what looked like a mug that was all rough and uneven. Dark green with a ridge round the top – you know – a bit battered.' Michael grinned into the camera.

'If I could just turn to Northamptonshire's County Curator, Janet Wilberforce: could you tell me what happened next? How did you get involved?'

Mrs Wilberforce's great face filled the screen, her eyes flicking suspiciously at the lens, and then: 'These two clever boys phoned me at home a couple of Saturdays ago and explained what they'd found and where it was.'

'Did you guess at the significance of the find, at that time?'

Mrs Wilberforce smiled; a few wisps of white hair

lifted in the breeze. Out of focus, but behind her, they could see the movement of a yellow digger, bumping over the beaten-up ground, its grabbing arm held aloft like a praying mantis.

'I had my – ah, suspicions,' – and she smiled as if about to reveal a secret. 'You see, the boys had pulled out of the mud an old, corroded drinking tankard. The kind that would have been popular in ale-houses at any time during the past three hundred years.

'But this one was different—'

He picked up his pen.

The house is important to me, something special because me and my mum and dad have made it our own, so that the way it smells, the way it creaks at night, the fact that the kitchen window sticks in summer, all that kind of thing make it important to me, like it's a part of my life. And to lose it will be like saying goodbye to an old friend.

They'd sat in the lounge, spread out on the sofa, watching the early evening news. His father staring intently at the screen, his glasses slipped loose from their rest on the bridge of his nose. Worry about the magazine – about getting it to the printers on time – carved into the sharp cut of his jaw; the grip of his hand on the chair.

His mother on the other side, sipping a mug of coffee, a faint smile touching her lips. 'You spoke like a professional,' she said, 'clear and confident.'

Mrs Wilberforce said: 'It took a couple of days to soak away the copper corrosive products to reveal the silver plating underneath but here it is.'

And with that she held up to the camera, less bulky now, and pitted and dull, the old broken-down tankard; still leaning to the side, but now more of the shadow of what it once had been.

'And there's some writing engraved on it?'

'Yes,' she said. 'The boys spotted the date, low down by the base, but everything else was masked by corrosion.'

'Well, what does it say?'

'Here – Michael – you're the one who pulled this out, you explain what it says.'

He held the tankard tenderly and looking into the camera, into their home, said: 'Mrs Wilberforce said that John Clare didn't go to regular school and that, didn't have books about the place, but he was a good writer, and when his first book of poems was published, in 1820, he was really famous – like a pop star or something.

'All his life was a struggle — what with being short of money and having a large family. And even his skill was a problem because his publisher and other people — they wanted his language tidied up — made more orderly.' A shy grin: 'You know, spelt properly.'

'It says here,' and he pointed to the place, '"Presented to John Clare, Poet. On the pub-pub-lication of Poems De-scriptive of Rur-al Life and Scenery, by his friends and admirers. 1820."'

'And if you turn the tankard round . . .' said Mrs Wilberforce, pointing.

'Yeah,' said Michael, 'you can see four lines of poetry that Mrs Wilberforce says were written about this place,' — and here Michael half-turned so that the trees and pond and grass, still glinting with the late rain, came into focus. He said:

'"Hope's sun is seen of every eye
The halo that it gives
In nature's wide and common sky
Cheers every thing that lives"'

'Thank you, Michael. So, we're standing on the heath where John Clare came throughout his life and on which he based some of his writing?'

Mrs Wilberforce nodded, smiling. 'Yes, this was very important—'

'Still is,' said Michael. 'Still is.' Pushing into the conversation, head tilted, eyes defiant; forcing his face into the camera. Mrs Wilberforce shoved aside, eyebrows arrowed in surprise.

'This great place was important to Clare,' said Michael, 'and for – all of us. It's wild and – you know – not developed or anything. Just trees and grass and wildlife. And' – pointing – 'if your camera looks over there – this place will soon be a building site. There's already diggers and bulldozers and that. Scraping the vegetation away, shifting earth.'

To his right, Mrs Wilberforce standing with a faint downturn to her mouth. Interrupted, silent. Millicent Jones out of shot but nodding every now and then as Michael spoke. Like she was encouraging him. Tony remembered the light wind touching the grass; a blackbird watching from a fence post. And that fierce gust of anger.

'Very soon, all this,' – Michael's arm made a circling movement – 'everything here will be – gone. The trees will be gone; the tracks made by rabbits and hares and foxes. Wild flowers. All of it. Gone for ever. And then there'll be – hundreds of houses, garages, cars. Loads of concrete. So' – eyebrows drawn together

– 'if people want to see a bit of the country the old poet liked and wrote about, they'd better hurry up. Get on over – come and stand here.'

Twenty-six

Delaney didn't say anything that Thursday, when Tony arrived at school, Kevin Douglas shouting across the form room: 'Saw you on the telly, Hudson. You and Slater. You didn't look that much of a twat.' Everyone had laughed, although it turned out that only two people had caught the broadcast. Katie Street said she'd like his autograph as he was the only person she knew who had been on television.

Overall, when he looked back, the week had seemed to be cruising towards a gentle conclusion. All the excitement of their find and the television interview gradually subsiding into the routine of school: a comprehension in French, a commendation for his work on the character of Romeo from Mr Rolph; the dream of lunchtime as they trudged through Maths, Mr Thomas yelling: 'Equations are important. For all of you.'

And yet of course, it wasn't normal. It was like one

moment they were bumping along the tracks heading towards some vague destination – hidden away in the mist – and the next, they were at the top of a helter skelter, staring down an impossible drop, with the car beginning to tilt and someone behind starting to scream.

That Friday he'd said to Michael, 'I'll call round maybe,' as they crossed the water meadow, weaving away from the soft mud and puddles.

'OK, mate,' he'd said, peeling left. 'See you later.'

And he'd cycled up Durham and Edinburgh and then on across the traffic on the Stamford Road to the oasis of Drayton Park, the hill of Windsor Road and then the house with the new 'For Sale' sign, like the red blade of an old axe.

His mother looked up from the paper as he walked in. She didn't smile. She said: 'You're on the news, Tony.'

And at six o'clock, they'd all three of them sat watching the bulletin. At the end, a frozen piece of black-and-white footage of a woman standing in front of a digger, held like a margin to the left of the screen. The newscaster, Granville Berkley, looked into the camera and said: 'Protesters have halted work at a building site in the East Midlands. Workmen from the firm of Carmell Construction were forced to down tools as groups of demonstrators invaded the land proposed as the site of the new village of Castor Hanglands, situated on heathland west of Peterborough.'

The camera cut to a group of men and women who had joined hands and encircled a bulldozer. Like it was some kind of child's game, he thought. They were all young; wore jeans, old pullovers. One man had his hair in dreadlocks. He seemed to be dancing to some inner music, in front of that great cutting edge.

'. . . the protesters have been arriving throughout the day,' said Berkley, 'and have stopped development, in some instances by chaining themselves to machinery and trees, and elsewhere by setting up camp to prevent further work on the site.'

A woman with red hair tied with black ribbon stood in the bucket of a dumper truck. She swung a placard that said 'Free the Heath' in time to music coming from a cassette recorder sitting in the driver's seat. 'Free the Heath,' she chanted, as if it was a person falsely imprisoned. 'Free the Heath. Free the Heath. Free the Heath.'

Berkley said: 'The protest follows the pattern of similar demonstrations at Manchester Airport and at Newbury, where the bypass scheme was opposed over a period of years. We now go live to our reporter on the site, Peter Gosport.'

There was a shot of a raincoated figure looking into the camera, holding an earpiece. Berkley said: 'Peter, have the demonstrators made clear the purpose of the protest?'

'Oh yes. It seems to have been kicked off by the recent discovery of a silver tankard found in a nearby pond two weeks ago by two schoolboys. Apparently the tankard belonged to the 19th-century poet, John Clare, who was born at Helpston, just to the north of where I'm speaking.'

He thought of Michael waiting for him that Wednesday in the park, saying, 'We'll have to go back. You know that don't you?' like it was the most obvious thing in the world. Two weeks past and now this. He looked across at his father, his eyes narrow in concentration, head tilted against his hand.

'Clare was a bit of an environmentalist in his own right, and one of the boys – a – Michael Slater, speaking about their find on a Midlands TV news programme, made it quite clear that he disapproved of the destruction of this area, which, to tell the truth is an attractive and unspoilt stretch of rural Britain . . .'

And all that yellow machinery belonged to Carmell Construction: he leaned forward and stared into the screen. All those people – they worked for Carmell. The man with the polished voice. The company that

217

had killed Michael's dad. The man who had said: 'Is that a defaulter I see?'

'. . . I've been chatting to a few demonstrators, and it seems many of them read about the development on the internet. There are quite a few local people here, who don't want this bit of wilderness to be taken away.'

Back in the studio, Granville Berkley said: 'OK, thanks, Peter. That was Peter Gosport at Ailsworth Heath in the East Midlands. And now the main points of the news again.'

His father turned to him, a smile as faint as mist touching his face. He said: 'You'll have to let us see this great find, Tony. After all you went through.'

'Yes,' he said, smiling quickly; ambushed by this sudden interest. Thinking of that long day and the grey road and the brown woodland. Thinking of his father in the precinct, anger held by his mother's arm. Now this.

'I think Mrs Wilberforce was looking after the tankard for them,' his mother said. 'She had to find out whether the county had an interest in buying it.'

'Michael's got it,' he said. 'Mrs Wilberforce gave it back. On Wednesday. When we'd finished at the heath. I'll ask him to bring it round; so that you can have a look at it. And everything.'

'I'd like that,' his father said quietly, looking across

218

from his chair. 'Not because of the protest and the news and whatnot, but because of – you know – the risk you both took, that day.'

He went to bed thinking about his father and what he had said. And what that look had meant.

The following morning, as the time turned 10.17 on the oven clock, and as rain beat against the windows from a grey sky, he sat at the kitchen table looking into the blue eyes and spreading beard of Mr Raymond Barrow, who was saying: 'The traffic was pretty tedious until the Brackley turn-off and then everything seemed to lighten up.'

'Yes,' said Mrs Barrow. 'We seemed to lose most of the lorries and caravans by then,' and she laughed and sipped from her cup. Their curly-haired daughter nibbled from a biscuit and blushed whenever anyone looked at her.

It was cups and saucers today, he noticed. The usual clutter of mugs had been pushed away into the cupboard and the kitchen was heavy with the smell of coffee.

Mr Barrow said, 'And what do you do for a living?' looking across the table at his father.

'I'm in the magazine business,' he said, glancing up and trying on a smile. 'You know, a listings magazine for children and their families.'

'We have a circulation of about 40,000 copies,' his mother said. 'Distributed through primary schools. Across the county.'

'Right,' said Mr Barrow. 'That sounds really interesting.'

'Yes,' his father said. 'Perhaps you'd like to see round?'

And Tony slowly followed them through the house, listening to the Barrows talking about the views and saying that all the rooms were a 'good size' and that there seemed to be enough wall sockets.

'Someone's got an interest in aviation, I see,' said Mr Barrow, turning to smile as they cluttered his room, the little girl picking up a yo-yo he'd left on his desk.

'He's been building aircraft since we came here,' his mother said. And then: 'I'm strictly forbidden to dust them.'

Mrs Barrow said, 'I should think not!' and they'd all laughed and turned round and retraced their steps towards the stairs and the kitchen.

Outside, in the garden, it had stopped raining and his mother had hurried to fill one of the strange spaces that seemed to open up in the conversation. Like crevasses on the ice floe of chat, he thought. Great yawning gaps that everyone stood away from but were unable to fill or to cross, so that when his mother threw a bridge over the icy silence it was in the hope that everyone would be able to follow, not that the bridge would be kicked away and leave people stranded on either side.

She said: 'I don't know if you caught the news last night, but Tony was one of the boys who found John Clare's drinking mug over on Ailsworth Heath. A couple of weeks ago.'

And Mr Barrow turned from looking out over the industrial estate that winked and shone in the mid-morning sun. His thick eyebrows were drawn together and his face was suddenly serious. Like the sun suddenly covered by passing clouds, the industrial estate thrown into shadow.

'You mean the place that's been invaded by a group of rent-a-mob hooligans? I mean I obviously don't know anything about the mug but it seems to me,' – looking round the group – 'that people who challenge democratic decisions and who hinder legitimate business activities should be prosecuted.'

'With the full rigour of the law?' his father added, left eyebrow raised.

'Absolutely. You simply can't allow layabouts and scroungers and all the rest of the social lepers to overturn the law of the land.'

Twenty-seven

Monday morning. Four days before the end of term and he could feel the drizzle as he stood to mount the kerb at Drayton Park. A fine mist from a sky thick with cloud. There were bits of litter over by the bandstand – crisp packets and sandwich bags – and he guessed there had been a concert that last Sunday.

There were green shards of glass by the old phone box on Windsor Road, like brittle, late-flowering crocuses, and he quickly manoeuvred the bike on to the road to avoid a flat. Vandals, he thought. Smashing stuff up.

He swung left past the new houses opposite the bowling green and then right for the climb up Beech Farm Road.

It was just gone eight and there was no sign of students heading towards the community college, but a steady stream of cars passing him on their way to connect with the Stamford Road and the slow drive north.

At the junction, he stood waiting in the drizzle for the traffic to ease before crossing on to Weston Hill. It was a shade after 8.10 and he pressed through the gears to make the most of the descent into the valley of the Scratch Brook before the steep climb on the other side.

Sheep grazed among the ridges and furrows of the old field just beyond the hedge, and at one point, close to the bridge, he saw a weasel dash across the road.

Something to tell Michael, he thought. When he got to his house.

Like the phone call on Saturday afternoon.

He'd been upstairs in his room, fixing the undercarriage on the Kittyhawk, when his mother called from the lounge: 'Tony – phone!'

And when he'd lifted the receiver, Miss Wilson, the Head of Year, said: 'Tony? Sorry to bother you over the weekend, but you'd already gone when I tried to catch you yesterday.'

Her voice sounded warm and concerned.

'I waited for Michael. On the Year 7 playground,' he said, suddenly breathless; his words tripping and stumbling as if he were climbing a mountain.

'Right. Well just after I'd seen his report card, Mrs Stein rang through to tell me the *Gretford Mercury* were trying to set up an interview with you both. On Monday morning.'

'Oh,' he said. 'At school, you mean?'

'Yes. At school. About eleven.'

'All right.'

'But I've not been able to contact Michael: could you let him know about this?'

'OK.'

'And, Tony – could you bring the tankard to school with you? – I'm assuming that you've still got it?'

'Oh – yes – yes – it's at Michael's house. I'll tell him.'

'Good,' she said. 'It'll make a nice picture.'

'Everything all right?' his mother had called. 'That was a teacher I assume?'

'Yeah – it's fine, Mum,' he'd said. 'Just funny talking to her. That's all. At home and everything.'

But when he'd cycled over on Sunday afternoon, to see Michael, no one was in. The old caravan was still beached on the drive and a bottle of washing-up liquid stared from the kitchen window, but neither Michael nor his mum answered the repeated taps he made on the back door.

And then, of course, there was his father. He'd spent most of the weekend, once the Barrows had departed, up in his bedroom with the door closed. But when Tony had gone out to the shed to fetch his bike his father had been standing there, arms loose by his side, looking up at the old tourer hanging from the rack on the wall.

'OK, Dad?' he'd said, feeling embarrassed. Like he'd walked in on something he shouldn't be seeing.

'Fine,' his father had said in a faint, flat voice that was hard to hear. As if he were talking from a distance. And then he'd said, as Tony made a move to squeeze past: 'They were terrible people, Tony. The Barrows.' And he turned his grey face towards the door. 'No generosity at all.'

But then again, that wasn't really something he could discuss with Michael. His father just seemed very tired and he supposed it was all the work of the magazine and the worry over money.

He turned off Weston Lane just before the garden centre, the three flags hanging limp in the rain, and pushed down the hill, past the Shoemaker's Tavern and the small supermarket, before turning into Durham Avenue. People were coming out to their cars and there was a queue building at the bus stop. He wondered whether Michael would be still in bed.

Four minutes later he waited while his friend

spooned cereal into his mouth, bits of milk dribbling away from his bottom lip.

'Sheesaidwah?' he asked, looking up.

'You know. Interview with the *Mercury*. There's someone coming to school. This morning.'

'Yeah?'

'She wanted you to bring the tankard. You know. For the picture?'

'OK – it's upstairs,' Michael said, no longer eating. 'What else?'

'You didn't see the news. On Friday night?'

Michael shook his head.

'So you don't know. That we were mentioned? On the news?'

'You're joking – what did they say?'

Tony looked at his watch. It was just gone half past. 'We'll have to be going, Michael.'

'Yeah – all right,' getting up to drop his dish into the sink. 'Just tell me – what happened. On the telly.'

Michael stuffed a packet of sandwiches into his bag and then plucked three pound coins from the teapot on the sideboard, and Tony told him about the last item, and how the reporter had mentioned their find and had even referred to Michael by name.

'My name?' he said. 'Michael Slater?' turning the key in the back door before getting his bike from the shed.

226

And then, as they cycled on to Brighton: 'Old mother Stein can't have seen that else she wouldn't have set up an interview. You know, not with the protesters and that.'

They pushed up the hill and then crossed over to pick up the path between the houses and the back way to school. It was as they approached the church on the green, opposite the allotments, that Michael suddenly eased on the brakes, and said: 'You've told your parents, and that. About our great skive. That Friday?'

And when he'd said that he had, Michael said, 'OK then, well when this person from the paper appears: let's go for it. Tell everything. How does that sound?'

It sounded frightening.

The truth to his parents was one thing, but now the truancy, the forged note, the lies – how would that feel if the paper printed their story?

'Why? What's the point?' he asked, drawing level.

Michael was silent, his head bent, looking down at the road below the crossbar.

'Our story. Our adventure, mate. Why pretend any more that we got hold of the tankard as if by magic? Remember that copper, back when we were stopped and that? What did he say – that we were courageous and all that. We speak for ourselves, in our own way. Not let others tell it for us.'

227

And he looked across at Tony, a wide smile embracing his face. 'C'mon, Tone – my ideas haven't been too wrong so far, have they?'

Twenty-eight

Truant Protest

A truant and an excluded pupil started the Ailsworth Heath protest, it emerged last night.

Michael Slater and Tony Hudson, both 14, and attending Scratch Brook Community College in Northamptonshire, used a school day to cycle to the Heath in search of a poet's lost beer mug.

Their find of John Clare's tankard led to an impassioned plea by Slater to protect the site against developers.

'It's important to save the countryside,' he said yesterday, 'not build all over it.'

Mrs Isobel Stein, headteacher of Scratch Brook, commented that she was disappointed that Tony Hudson had truanted, although she was delighted with what had been recovered.

In the north of the county, police have refused further access to the heath. Inspector Charles Cork said yesterday: 'There are over 500 demonstrators on the site and a significant number are from the local community.

'However, in the interests of public safety it's important that the protest is strictly controlled.'

Twenty-nine

'What does Michael know?' he thought, the paper stretched over his handlebars among the long shadows of Drayton Park. Dark fingers reaching from the lime trees, the air turning cold.

Not our story at all. Just names. The excluded pupil and the truant. And Mrs Stein? She knew the right words to say. She was 'disappointed'.

No one had mentioned the story in the *Express* until he was heading away from the cycle shed at the end of school. He was thinking about going into town when the kid from Year 10 yelled after him: 'Hey, you're Hudson, aren't you? You're in the paper.' And he'd waved the *Express* at him.

'Been out skiving with Michael Slater, then?' he'd said, grinning. 'See old mother Stein thought it were a bit of a laugh.'

They'd told their story to the woman from the *Mercury* and had their picture taken and he expected to see something appear that night, or at least in the next week. But not in a national paper. That hadn't been the arrangement.

'You can have it,' the kid said. 'Cut out and keep.'

'Thanks,' he said. 'Thanks a lot.'

His mother dried her hands and looked at the story.

'Hmm,' she said. 'Difficult to recognise you from this. I don't know what Michael was playing at to trust the press. But then he's only fourteen. As it says in the report. I wouldn't fret. Most people forget about small stories like this. They've got too much to worry about in their own lives.'

Like Dad, he thought. The figure in the bedroom who slept in fits during the day, his face grown long and bearded; his eyes far back in their sockets.

'Do you think Dad should see a doctor or something?' he said.

'I think so,' his mother said, reaching over and switching on the oven. 'I think he probably will.'

'Is it all to do with work and that?'

'That's right. And the fact that the business hasn't succeeded and that we've got to move. He feels—'

'It's all his fault?'

'Yes – something like that.'

'But why don't we tell him it's not his fault? It's

those people who owe us. They're to blame.'

She smiled and ruffled his hair. 'You're a good boy – to think of your dad like that. On one level I think he does understand, but deep down he doesn't believe it.' She sighed and smiled. 'I'll have another bash at persuading him. To go down to the surgery.'

Katie Street said: 'Did you really skive school to find that mug?'

'Yeah,' he said, smiling. 'It was a long way.'

Susan Moore and Anita Chauda staring at him on the Year 9 playground.

'My dad showed me it in the paper,' Katie went on. 'I'd never have guessed – that it was you.'

'No,' he said. Feeling stupid.

'I know Slater's your friend but – I'd have thought you'd have had more sense.'

He shrugged. He said: 'We had no other way – to get to the heath – find the mug.'

The bell outside the library rang and it was time to go in to morning registration. Listen to the comments from Delaney and Kevin Douglas. Note the raised eyebrow from Mr Rolph when he answered his name in the register. But Miss Wilson didn't appear. There was no call to go down and see Mrs Stein.

'Her car's not in the car park,' Michael said, as they

walked down the corridor. 'Probably off on her holidays.' And then: 'What can they do anyway? We got the tankard – that's important. Not this – cack.' Chin stuck out, head tilted – ready for anything.

And much later, after he'd played around with maths problems as interesting as cold pasta, had worked with Chris Phillips in Science – after the hours of lessons had trickled past like a tired stream in summer, he'd said goodbye to Michael and cycled home.

Up in his room he stared down at the model of the Kittyhawk. It sat on its three wheels and looked as if it was ready to taxi into the paint shop. He turned it round slowly by the edge of one wing, looking at the gaping shark's-mouth air intake, the broad curve of the tailplane, the gentle dihedral of the wings.

Stockier than the Spitfire, he thought, with its shorter length and thickened waist, but strong and rugged like a middle-weight boxer.

Would there be time to apply the dusty desert camouflage, he wondered, or any point in attaching it by black cotton to the ceiling, imagining it climbing to join the others.

But then his mum was at the bottom of the stairs and shouting: 'Tony: news.'

'It's about Ailsworth Heath,' she said, standing by the door.

The local politician, Haydon Jones, was already talking into the camera: '. . . three and a half thousand dwellings will take some of the pressure off Peterborough. These people, who probably don't complain about their handouts from the state, would be much better occupied getting paid employment and helping to build a strong economy.' And then, suddenly, there was the face of Jocelyn Carmell. Hair hidden beneath a light brown cap, the collar of an oiled jacket turned up against the rain. He looked sternly into their room, his grey eyes glinting in the light.

He said: 'This thing is clearly out of order. I've got chaps on this site who haven't been able to do any work for the past six days. I can quite understand people's anxieties, but the proper planning procedures have been followed. To the letter.

'And I've also got to say, having glanced at some of the reports in the press this week, that I find it distinctly unpalatable that this whole sorry saga should have begun as a result of two pupils from a Gretford comprehensive. One of whom had numerous exclusions as a result of violent conduct. And we're supposed to take all this seriously,' – and he pointed a despairing arm in the direction of the tents and the fires and the huddled figures sheltering beneath the grey branches of the old ash trees.

'If we're heading for another Newbury – and God forbid – then my company for one will simply go out of business. And the people here will lose their jobs. There's a shortage of homes in this area and it's up to local government to meet that need wherever it can.'

In the silence of the turned-off set, he asked: 'What did he mean by "unpalatable"?'

'It's got absolutely nothing to do with you or Michael. Those, those comments – were – disgraceful.' His mother's face was red and her eyes looked fierce. She pulled at the drying-up towel, squeezing and tugging at the damp cloth. 'That man is – an – absolute – disgrace.' And then, coming across and putting a hand on his shoulder. 'You simply ignore what he says. I'll go back into the kitchen and write Mrs Stein a letter about it. You simply can't go on national television and expect to get away with saying things like that.'

Later he went to bed, stepping quietly past the door closed on his sleeping father.

Thirty

'As you can see, there's a spacious dining-room and lounge with a gas fire to supplement the radiators. Plenty of light from the bay window there, and the furniture, although not in the first flush of youth, is entirely serviceable.'

'Right,' his mother said. 'And the street is quiet.'

'Yes. You'll find that a major change from Scotton Road. A haven of peace here.' Mr Yorke turned and smiled.

His father stood still and stared around. The drop of his head and the down-turn of his shoulders gave him a hunched look. Like a child's bear that had been dragged around the house too many times. He was silent and Tony noticed the razor cut on his chin, the bit of stubble that he'd missed on his cheek.

'Shall we move on?' asked Mr Yorke, looking at them all. 'Have a look at the kitchen?'

It wasn't the worn brown wallpaper in the lounge

that bothered him, nor the fingerprints smeared on the bathroom mirror. The attic bedroom, with the ceiling cut into strange angles and the view across the garden, was, if anything, more exciting than his own room, but that was the point really. It wasn't his own, not the place that he'd grown to know and be a part of.

When he opened his eyes in the morning he knew immediately, without thinking, where the light was coming from, what the noise from the radio downstairs meant. On Mondays he would lie in bed and hear the slow progression of the bin-men heading towards their house and late on Friday nights he'd sometimes be awoken by the stray drunks shouting abuse as they made their way out of town.

But number 3 Croydon Gardens wasn't like that. It would be quieter; the fall of light would be different; the route to school would change; and none of the furniture was their own. He wasn't even sure that he'd be allowed to unpack his aircraft. Not even sure that he'd want them flying in this strange sky.

As they drove across town, the car silent with their thoughts, they passed the sign for Scratch Brook and his thoughts were pulled back to that last meeting four days before. The secretary from the front office searching the class for his face before asking Mr Rolph: 'Mrs Stein would like to see Tony Hudson.'

She said: 'I've received a letter from your mother, Tony, about Mr Carmell's interview on television last night. Although I didn't see the news myself, I understand that he made some remarks that could have referred to you and Michael Slater.

'I will be writing to your mother in full, and I will pass on the points she makes to Mr Carmell. However, this is to say that the school is disappointed that you saw fit, in your interview with the *Mercury* on Monday, to advertise the fact that you had truanted on the Friday you cycled to Ailsworth Heath and presumably' – here picking up a sheet of A4 – 'that you forged your mother's signature to conceal your actions.

'Although you recovered a valuable artefact – and I believe two museums are interested in purchasing it – the fact is that you simply acted without properly considering the implications of your behaviour. For instance, you could quite easily have been injured during the course of the cycle ride.

'And as for Michael, his boastful – and I can think of no other word – acknowledgement of your actions places this school in an unfavourable light.

'With reference to the business at Ailsworth Heath, I can understand the different points of view that have been voiced during the past week and I have no wish to revisit that particular debate. I will say, however, that I feel it was particularly provocative of Michael to give his opinion when interviewed by Midlands TV. The programme was interested in the tankard you found, not his anxieties about the environmental issues at stake.

'Now I'm sorry, on this last day before the Easter break, to have to speak to you so directly, but I – and Miss Wilson – feel – that it's important that we make our position entirely clear to you about your conduct in this whole affair.

'Do you understand what I've said?'

'Mrs Stein,' he said quietly, his voice like dry paper. 'I'm sorry for truanting – and the letter. There were things going on that made it difficult for us. But we did our best to act – well – properly. I've told my parents about everything. And as for the heath, we – that's Michael and me – we think what's going on is – it's wrong – and well, you should go there and see, have a look for yourself. Then you'd . . . understand . . .'

His voice lost itself amongst the books and the filing cabinet and the pale wood of the office furniture. He quickly looked down at the unmoved face of the woman staring up at him.

'That's as maybe, but I've made my – the school's – position entirely clear. Now, if you could get back to your form room, I have to prepare my address to the sixth form.'

When the car pulled up outside the house, his parents sat quietly staring ahead, his mother reaching out to cover his father's clenched fist.

She said: 'We'll live to fight another day, you know.'

And after a while, after a silence so long a flock of starlings completed a circle in the northern sky, his father said: 'I do know that.' And then leaning forward and pointing: 'Isn't that Michael Slater over there?'

The figure in the green tracksuit top and blue jeans, face drawn back in a smile, waved at them from the Windsor Road turning and moments later, crossing in front of a white hire van, was leaning red-faced into the passenger window.

'Hiya!' he said. 'I've brought the tankard. So that you can see it before Ma Wilberforce takes it away. To get it valued.'

'That's really thoughtful of you,' said his mother. 'You must stay for lunch.'

And so they sat round the kitchen table, with the radio murmuring and the old mug tilted amongst the bread rolls and cheese and tomatoes. And Michael explaining to his father what it felt like to remove his trainers and tread on the leaf-soft bed of the pond, through water as sharp as an electric shock.

'I saw my dad do the same once,' Michael said. 'But in the summer. Where I'd snagged a line across the other side of a stream. Didn't think twice about getting in over his knees.

'Just laughed and said it was a bit of a cold 'un!'

He heard the sound of wheels on gravel outside, crunching as though through broken glass, and he thought somewhere that it would be next door's daughter returning for her lunch or for some of her accounting stuff, but then they heard a foot kick the door scraper. There was a short pause and then the bell rang sharply.

'I'll get it,' he said, pushing his chair back against the alcove wall.

He could see the outline of a dark coat and white shirt through the frosted glass. Like a businessman, he thought. Or a religious salesman. He reached up and turned the catch, pulling on the door – and looked into the grey eyes of Jocelyn Carmell.

'Hello,' he said. 'Are your parents at home?'

Thirty-one

He went back into the kitchen where Michael was saying: 'Yeah. My father was really keen on coarse fishing. Bought me a pike rod just before he died.'

Tony said, 'Mr Carmell is at the door. He'd like to talk with you,' looking across at his parents.

'And I think I'd like to talk with him,' said his mother, getting up and untying her apron. 'I won't be a moment.'

She went out to the hall, her shoes tap-tapping across the tiles.

'Mrs Hudson? Jocelyn Carmell,' they heard. 'I've called round to offer you an apology for my indiscretions of the other day. On the television. And to discuss with you a matter of pressing and – I hope – mutual importance. Without prejudice, you understand.'

In the silence Tony looked across at the tankard, at the old scar in its side and at the inscription that was as

243

faint as a line of birds flying into a winter sky.

Michael reached out and touched it with his forefinger.

'Well, you'd better come in then. But I must say, Mr Carmell, that we are very angry about what you said. That simply wasn't called for. To refer to my son and to Michael Slater – as though they were simply yobs.'

'Quite so, and that's the reason – ah, hello,' he said, as he came into the kitchen, looking around the table. 'I hope this isn't an inconvenient moment?'

'No, we're a bit late, but we've mostly finished,' his mother said. 'My husband – David. Tony you've already met and—'

'We know each other,' said Michael. 'We've already passed the time of day.'

Outside he could see the faint coat of green on the forsythia; the branches alive with sparrows. In the silence he could hear the sound of the stone-mason: *chip-chip, chip-chip, chip-chip.*

But now the air suddenly stank of cedar and cigar smoke. Spreading across the kitchen like an oil slick.

His mother coughed and said: 'It might be easier, Mr Carmell, if we were to go and talk about whatever it is somewhere else. In the lounge maybe.'

'That sounds very sensible, Mrs Hudson. And perhaps Mr Hudson would care to join us?'

Again the silence. The conversation tripping on sudden stones.

'David?' she said.

His father looked up, his face pale and his shoulders hunched. 'Yes,' he said. 'I'll come.' Slowly pushing back his chair and leaning into the wall, his hand lightly touched Michael's arm as he passed.

'Perhaps you two could wash up?' his mother said. 'We'll have the pudding later.'

'All hands on deck,' said Carmell, smiling. 'It's important to take part in the mundane chores.'

'Right,' she said, her face suddenly bunched into a frown. 'If you'd like to follow me.'

'It takes a moment or two for the water to run hot,' Tony said. 'Something to do with the length of the pipes.'

They worked in silence, Michael dropping scraps into the bin while he shoved the cold food back in the fridge. He could see Michael's bike against the fence, attached by a security cable. Like the fence on the heath, where they'd stood looking at the sign that announced the extinction of the land – Michael spotting the prints of Carmell Construction.

They could hear the murmur of voices down the

corridor. The door firmly closed and the sound lost whenever a car passed on the main road.

He waited for Michael to lift a bowl from the drainer.

'Probably going to offer us compensation,' he said.

Michael didn't answer: went on polishing the bowl, looking down.

Water slooshed off a plate; a piece of tomato floated in the grey. Tony felt for the cutlery at the bottom; wiped each knife clean of grease. Stacked them in the holder by the washing-up liquid. Listened to the hum of the fridge; the hiss of the boiler.

Michael said: 'That letter we received. That time after my dad was killed, said: "Although we in no way admit liability, we would wish to extend our greatest sympathies to you and to your son, over this tragic accident."'

Tony knew he was quoting from memory.

'Maybe my dad was too close to the vehicle, who knows? But not having brake lights? That must count for something. Not just lying, poncy words.' He looked at Tony, his face without expression. 'Compensation!'

They put away the plates and sat at the table, listening to the distant drone of bees.

'I didn't know they'd have so much to talk about. To each other,' Tony said. But then the door opened and his father was standing in the kitchen breathing as though he'd run across from the Scratch Brook estate.

He said: 'Mum and myself would like you to come and take part in the discussion. Although it's complicated, it concerns us all.'

'Me as well?' said Michael.

'You more than anyone,' said his father.

There was a slight flush to Carmell's face, he noticed, taking a seat on the sofa with Michael. His head was leaning against his hand; worry creasing his forehead.

When he'd come to school and handed out the commendations and when he was looking down at him as he collected litter from the rose garden, he cast a shadow like a tall building. A dark figure with sharply cut hair and a bright tie. A voice as clear and as smooth as the olive oil his father ladled across green salad.

But now, in their house, sagging in the corner of the chair, everything seemed changed. Like the scattering of leaves in November changes the shape of a tree.

His mother was speaking. She said: 'Mr Carmell has been talking to us about Ailsworth Heath. As you know, his company has been awarded the contract to develop the site—'

Michael leaned forward. He said: 'Is that what's meant by hacking down trees – filling in ponds?

247

Burying all the wildlife under piles of bricks?'

Carmell looked down at the gas fire, his hand rubbing his mouth. Like someone using sandpaper, he thought.

'Just a second, Michael. I know you're angry – but I do need you to listen carefully to what Mr Carmell is going to say to – all of us. Then we'll have a chance to talk about it. Share our ideas. Is that OK? All right then,' and she looked across the fire. 'I think you can explain to everyone what you have in mind.'

'Right. Well this is all rather complicated but if I could make it as clear as possible for everyone concerned,' – his hand lightly raised in their direction. 'I'd just like to sketch out – explain – what I think are the key issues at stake in the north of the county. And you two – Michael and Tony – you were the boys responsible for starting the whole process,' – a slight laugh 'filling my building site with a collection of very angry people.'

He smiled across at them; his voice soft, his words lightly touching points of interest.

'However, I think it's very probable – in the next month – that an eviction order will be granted against the trespass – the demonstrators on the heath. That means bailiffs – officials appointed by the court – will come to the site and the protesters will be removed.

The police will stand by to make sure that the safety of everyone is secured.'

His father was leaning forward, listening closely; Michael looked up at the clock on the mantelpiece, watched the second hand as it slowly ticked round the dial.

Carmell coughed. He said: 'That is what happened in the cases of Manchester Airport and the Newbury bypass. Two other large-scale demonstrations against construction work. If that were to occur then absolutely nothing would have been achieved.'

He let his words hang in the silence. He reminded Tony of Mr King, back in primary school, when some kids in Year 6 had kicked a football through the staff room window. He'd spoken to the whole school in assembly, allowing the silences to gather around each of his warnings. Clouds without thunder.

'. . . all the sacrifice of the protesters would come to nothing. A great deal of public money would have been wasted. And so would everyone's time, including that of the police. So, why am I concerned about all this? Why should I have travelled over today to explain to you the seriousness of the situation?'

Carmell was sitting straighter now, turning to stare around the room, his eyes glancing at each of them. Brow furrowed, eyebrows pushed together. Someone trying to explain something really complicated. Wanting to help.

'Well, I'm obviously worried that my plant – the earth-moving equipment and so on – and labour – aren't tied up doing nothing.' He paused and smiled at his father. 'I have my own cash-flow problems to think about. I have other contracts that need attending to – I'm not in a position to sit on my hands. If I were to do so, to wait and see what happens, then my business would suffer and people might lose their jobs.

'I've discussed the whole issue with the landowner, Mr Priestly – been over to Peterborough – to see if it's possible to work out a compromise that would suit everyone. You know, the good old English way of give and take.'

There was a hint of a smile as he looked around the room. Tony's mother holding firm to the arm of the sofa; his father leaning back in his chair. Michael stared out of the window at the back garden.

'What I've agreed with the landowner is this: if the protesters could be persuaded to leave the heath, within the next ten days, then a twelve-acre site will be preserved outside the new village of Hanglands as a field centre. Mr Priestly is prepared to pay for the construction of an appropriate building with study areas and washrooms and so on, that would be made available to the public and to schools to enable proper research into the local environment. A considerable improvement on the non-existent facilities currently available, you'll have to agree. We felt it appropriate that a such a centre might be named in honour of the presiding genius of the region, John Clare.'

He paused, looking down, turning his wedding ring between thumb and forefinger. Allowing his ideas to sink in; making sure that the convoy was travelling at the same speed. Tony wondered what a field centre might be, and he also knew that Carmell was coming to the main point of the meeting. The reason he'd travelled over to visit them. He knew that if he looked up he would meet the gaze of those cold grey eyes.

'It's going to be difficult to bring to an end such a well publicised and deeply felt demonstration. We can talk to representatives of the groups, and we will do so. But we felt it would help the process, kick-start it, so to speak, were Michael and Tony to publicly endorse our suggestion. That is, to explain in their own words how the proposed field centre would answer some of the anxieties of the protesters.

'Obviously this would take up their time and cause inconvenience, but to demonstrate my appreciation of their efforts, my company would be prepared to award Michael an educational grant of two thousand pounds

– to help support him through his studies at Scratch Brook . . .'

Michael didn't shift his gaze from the back garden; didn't move his head to return the look from Carmell. He seemed to be watching the sparrows and the forsythia bush; the balance of a blackbird on the wooden fence. The pattern of clouds in the western sky.

'. . . and in the case of Tony and his family, to take out a series of full page, three-colour adverts, in Mr Hudson's magazine, up to a value of five thousand pounds. I know this is complicated, but we feel there is urgency to get the matter resolved as quickly as possible.'

You could hear the *swish-swish* of cars on the Scotton Road and there came from across the valley the hooting call of a train travelling to London. He thought of the new house in Croydon Gardens, with its smell of cooked food and unwashed clothes. The scuffed wallpaper and cigarette burns on the carpet. And he thought also of his bedroom and the aircraft and the view out over the industrial estate and the way the light flashed off traffic on the Northampton Road.

Michael said, 'We're to give a TV interview – is that right?' looking up at Carmell. 'And we'd say that because of your – your – idea – this study place – because of that – the protesters should pack up – go home. And then' – staring directly at the school governor – 'you can go ahead and smash up Ailsworth Heath? That's right, isn't it?'

Carmell looked down, his face reddening. He said, 'You're twisting my words,' coughing lightly into his hand. 'We're simply trying to find a compromise.'

Would the money – the five thousand pounds for the adverts – be enough to prevent their house being sold? If they agreed, would they be able to stay in their home?

His father looked down, hands locked in a kind of fierce prayer.

His mother said: 'Mr Carmell, I think you've made your position very clear. I think we need to – to talk over your ideas and call you in the next day or so. Tell you what we think.'

He stood up, straightening his jacket. He said: 'I should be very grateful, Mrs Hudson. And I would like to thank you all for being so patient and for listening so carefully as I outlined the complications of this difficult situation. I'm sure that we'll find some mutually agreeable solution.'

Carmell looked down at each of them, pulling on his coat. A tall man with silver hair; face marbled red and grey.

'I'll see you out,' said Tony's mother.

Again the delicate smile, the light wave of his hand. 'Good day,' he said.

Thirty-two

He bent his head into the wind that was coming in gusts from the right; last year's grass bedded yellow by the roadside. Up ahead, Michael steering into the bend, the dog-leg before Hannington. He could hear the hiss of tyres behind, and saw the fields, with their borders of elder and hawthorn, stretch away to the woods of Titchmarsh and Snapes.

There was an old tyre half-submerged in the pond on the corner and he knew that by May it would be speckled with duckweed, gently rising and falling in the shadow of willow.

When Mr Carmell had gone his mother came back into the lounge. She said: 'Well, there's a surprise: the big man not only comes to visit us, but also apologises and offers us money.'

She sat down.

'What do you think?'

He thought of the bills piled by the bread bin; the

stack of invoices his father was preparing, the brown envelopes tumbling over each other on the table in the dining-room. And he thought of this sudden flurry of bank notes. Like snow in August.

'We'd have to give an interview,' he said, 'simply go along with Mr Carmell's idea? About the nature centre and everything?'

'Yes.'

'And then we'd get the money – and Michael would receive two thousand pounds?'

'Yes.'

He could hear some kids shouting as they went past outside, the sound of a can being kicked along the pavement. He thought of the heath, with its pond and stream; dragonflies in the summer and great clumps of frogspawn in the spring. There was their house and the familiar routes to school; his room with its aircraft and magazines; the distant roofs out of the window and the noise from the street.

Michael was silent. He stared down and tugged at a loose thread in his jeans.

His father coughed.

He said: 'This affects all of us. But in a way it's easier for Rebecca and myself.' He looked at them, forehead tugged into a frown. 'Maybe I'm missing something, but I think there's only two people who can make the decision. Michael and Tony cycled north and found the tankard: they're old enough to say what should happen.'

Silence lapped the edge of the room, pushed them apart.

He looked across at the old crack in the wall, following its crooked path beside the mantelpiece as it headed south and then made its familiar turn towards the carpet.

His mother said: 'Why don't we all return tomorrow morning and Michael and Tony can come to a conclusion?' And then: 'Say, meet here at ten o'clock. How does that sound?'

There was a crow up ahead, feeding from some red mess smeared by the verge. As Michael approached it lifted off like a jagged piece of night. Tony watched it circle the dark branches of sycamore and then land, stiff-winged. Like a carrier pilot, he thought, putting down in a big swell.

Sometimes when he lay in bed on a Saturday or Sunday, just lying there and listening to the sounds of the house or the passing of cars, he would hear the scrape of starlings on the guttering above his window, and he knew they'd be wandering along, a few steps at a time, their heads jerking this way and that as they stared down into the garden.

But that morning, when he'd woken, it hadn't been like that. The starlings were elsewhere and his thoughts were filled with the heath and the house and his father.

And later, there'd been the soft drop of letters on the mat, his mother's footsteps on the stairs, not pausing and turning into her bedroom, but coming down the corridor to where he lay.

She said: 'There's a letter for you, Tony. Northampton postmark.'

He sat up and leaned back against the headboard; his mother drew the curtains.

It was one of those window envelopes, like his father used, but this one was white, his name and address in clear black type.

It felt bulky. There were several sheets of paper inside.

'Well go on,' she said, smiling. 'Open it.'

Dear Tony and Michael,

Wonderful news about your discovery. My colleague, Roger Baines, over in Peterborough, has made a search of the surviving correspondence in the John Clare collection and he's found a letter that explains how the tankard found its way on to Ailsworth Heath.

It connects to a very low period in Clare's life, although of course after his early success, he spent forty years chasing a dream.

In 1832, twelve years after the publication of his first book, Clare and his family (and there were eight children by this time), found themselves in serious financial difficulties. In fact they owed two years' rent on their house and were forced to leave Helpston.

They moved to the village of Northborough, a few miles away, and although this doesn't sound very serious, to a sensitive man like Clare, it was pretty devastating. You get a feeling of his unhappiness in a poem he wrote some time after the event. I don't know if you're familiar with it, but here are the first few lines:

'I've left mine old home of homes
Green fields and every pleasant place
The summer like a stranger comes
I pause and hardly know her face'

Although this was obviously put together at a later date, you get the feeling of considerable grief.

What is closer to the event is a letter he wrote to his friend, Eliza Emmerson, in London. He explains his worry about leaving Helpston and he comments on some poems he'd been writing. You then get this:

'I have to confes that in my sadnes at leaving the place I took a drink in the Blue Bell and then flusht with ale tramped the old road back to the heath In other times it would have gladened my heart to see the cowslaps again the path & the old heron lifting away into the sun but I came there as a gray clowd

I could not but think about my changd situation and in my low spirits I cast into the depths that old remembrance of former sucess I mean that fine silver quaffer so kindly given me by Messrs Taylor & Hessey

'I regret so rash an action to have abandoned so valued a trophy in a fit of sadness but there it is An uncommon gift casualy thrown away'

Obviously I'm delighted that my colleague has located this letter – based on my original hunch. I helped write the county guide to Clare Country a few years ago, and when you contacted me about the tankard, it rang a very loud bell about something I'd once read.

I hope you both find this of interest and I've included two photocopies of the original for you to keep. Needless to say, the existence of the letter will significantly enhance the value of your discovery.

I will be in touch with you nearer the time once the issue of ownership has been sorted out.

With best wishes
Janet Wilberforce

The road twisted left and then right, gradually climbing before the wood and the hill that took them down into Calderhay. He could see the rusted shape of an abandoned car up ahead, the bonnet gone and the grass burnt where there had been a fire. There were gulls walking among a field of new corn, and as they cycled so sparrows chased each other along the hedge.

When Michael arrived they'd sat around the kitchen table, the letter spread out and his father reading through the paragraphs, pausing every now and then as if to make sure they all understood, his eyes grown big behind his glasses.

And when it was over, when the letter was placed on the table in front of them, so he thought of the young man who had perhaps staggered along the dirt road one afternoon, the tankard hanging loose in his hand, and who had rested in the clearing by the pond as dark clouds filled his sky, and who had then flung his great prize in a wide arc across the water and watched it splash and vanish beneath that cold grey surface.

Michael said: 'So, we say yes to Carmell, and take the money; or we say no, and take the chance the heath will be destroyed anyway? That's it, isn't it?'

'Yes,' his father said quietly.

'Look,' said Michael. 'Don't let's mess about. Yeah, the

261

money would be great – I bet my mum would hack her arm off to get hold of two thousand – but I'm not going to. Carmell? – it would be shaking hands with Dad's killer.'

His face was red, like he got sometimes when Delaney gave him the needle. Bits of spit clinging to his bottom lip.

'What do you think, Tony?' his mother said quietly.

'Would the money save the house?' he asked, staring at the envelope. 'Would it prevent us from moving?'

'That's not at issue,' his father said. 'Not for discussion. You answer for yourselves.'

Tony looked up quickly, stared across at his father. Like there had been a sudden slip; like in winter where an icicle drops away and you know it's the beginning of a thaw. Answer for yourselves. He thought back to his room and the squadron, all the sights and sounds of home, everything they had put together over the years.

And the magazine: twenty-two months they had shared in the project – his father's brainchild – and now: answer for yourselves. His father had taken off his glasses, was looking across at him, leaning on his left hand. Michael was turned round, like he had when they were in the police car, when Tony had decided to tell the truth.

And he thought that their future – all of them – was

going to be decided by what he said next. That his father had given him the power to choose whether their house would be saved, whether the business could continue. They had been given a price.

He fingered the letter from Mrs Wilberforce, read again the words from the old poet – his sense of failure; his loss of home. Wouldn't he have taken the money – done anything to escape from his unhappiness? With his young family and great stack of bills?

But then he remembered the image of the hare crouched amidst the earth of the ploughed field. The story of the small boy wandering down the old road, looking for the edge of the world, and he took a deep breath and said: 'I think it's like it says here – like the heath is an "uncommon gift" and we shouldn't – shouldn't just allow it to be taken away – so that other people can make money.' His voice tailed off; he felt his face turn red. He looked down at the tufts in the green carpet.

'I'm not sure Mr Carmell would understand your thinking,' his mother said, smoothing the folds of her dress.

His father touched his arm. 'You've answered for all of us,' he said. 'And John Clare.'

It was just gone 10.32 by his watch as the thatch and stone of Calderhay came into view; the stubby church spire showing pale against the grey sky.

His father drew level. He yelled across: 'We'll stop at the bridge. In the village?'

He nodded.

At this rate they'd be in Helpston by two, he thought. They'd eat their sandwiches on the green by the memorial and then they'd cycle south into the sun, along the road to the dirt track, where the bulldozers and diggers and earthmovers were stalled.

'Come on,' Michael called back, 'you're like a pair of tortoises.'

They'd park their bikes against the fence and, although stopped by the police, they'd stand in the warmth and talk to the other demonstrators and look across the heath to the woodland. They'd point out the flash of yellow gorse to Dad; see the silver birch trees that led to the pond. Imagine the leeches swaying in the current.

And they'd wait for another spring.